Tempted by Fire

Erin Kellison

for my little dragons

CHAPTER 1

THE BONES OF A six-hundred-year-old skeleton lay on a wide, black laboratory table. Browned with time, they provided only a partial reconstruction of the individual's form. The feet were missing, the ribs were broken, and the long bones were splintered. But the characteristics that had drawn Thane Ryce Ealdian from his long seclusion were the extreme curvature of the spine, elongation of the phalanges, and the ridges along the frontal bone of the skull.

Dragon shifter. Absolutely.

A single glance at the bones and heat seared through Thane's body, so he looked away, giving his attention to

Dr. Buckley, the head osteology expert on the Kingman Hills archaeology project.

"We've become quite fond of her," Dr. Buckley said as he put on a pair of latex gloves. "Named her Anna after one of our team members who we lost during the dig."

Not Anna. Carreen. And Thane didn't care who they'd lost during the dig.

He swallowed his anger. Sometimes evidence of wounds survived the ages, even if the recipient did not. "Can you tell me how she died?"

"With remains this old, it's impossible to be sure, but there are a number of clues that help illuminate her last days."

Illuminate? Yes. With fire, if you please.

"She suffered a blow to the head near the time of death—there are no signs that any healing took place." Dr. Buckley lifted the skull to show a circular depression. "Blunt force, but I don't think it killed her. She was also struck here"—he indicated a rectangular hole, just to the side of the nasal cavity—"by a dagger or some other sharp implement. It too could have occurred near or shortly after death, to humiliate her or disfigure her face." Buckley looked up and met Thane's gaze, paled at what he found there, and quickly averted his eyes. He swallowed hard before continuing. "At the time, her deformities would've made her a pariah in her

2

community. The fourteen hundreds were particularly rough on shifters of all kinds. I'm surprised she lived to adulthood."

Thane took a deep breath through his gritted teeth. Not *deformed*. Carreen was clearly mid-shift when she died, therefore stronger, but also more vulnerable. Why she had attempted shifting at all, a woman who'd always denied the dragon within, was the mystery.

Dr. Buckley pointed to a long, thin indentation on the inside of her pelvis. "She also sustained a sharp force trauma here, most likely from a sword or dagger."

The room went hazy red. A slice like that to a woman of high birth could have only been intended to make absolutely certain she would bear no more heirs.

Thane looked up at Dr. Buckley, who took an immediate step back.

"Tell me about the infant."

"Of…of course." Dr. Buckley turned and retrieved a small metal tray from the shelf behind him. In the tray was a piece of skull, darker than the amber color of Carreen's remains. The few pieces of bone—what looked like a bit of spine, rib, and possibly leg—were splintered like driftwood.

"We can't determine the sex based on what we were able to retrieve," Dr. Buckley began.

Boy. It had been a boy named Rinc Ealdian. And now he was reduced to bones in a little metal tray. The child was six hundred years gone—six *hundred* years—and Thane still felt anger sparking the change in his blood. He breathed against it, concentrating on the chill of the laboratory and the smell of dirt that lightly permeated the air. Shifting now would solve nothing.

"The condition of the infant is even worse than Anna's—the female's, I mean," Dr. Buckley said. "These bones were burned, though it's impossible to ascertain if the burning occurred before or after death. As to the reason, the anthropologist on our team assures us that, again, the people of the time and their bias against shifters were likely responsible."

Thane didn't think so. The bias was more likely against the Ealdian bloodline. "There were objects found at the site, yes?"

There was one object in particular upon which everything hinged.

Dr. Buckley retrieved another tray. Inside it, a narrow white ruler separated the objects within. On one side rested a copper sigil, corroded brown and green, of entwined flying serpents. It clearly belonged to the Heolstor family, who were also claiming the remains as their own. On the other side of the tray were some bits of gold that Thane knew used to be earrings.

"The brooch was found in the female's hand," Dr. Buckley explained.

In her hand. Not merely near the body.

For the first time since Thane was alerted to the discovery of the remains, their provenance, and the fact that Heolstor was claiming them as kin, he cooled to ice. The brooch placed a Heolstor with Carreen at the time of her death. And if she had been mid-shift into a form she'd long repudiated, then something had awakened the dragon within her. Sometimes it happened that way for mothers defending their children.

"I still have to meet with the Heolstors"—Dr. Buckley paused to gulp, seeming to get his courage back up—"so I know that this might be a little premature, considering the claim hasn't been settled... But I'd like to take the opportunity to request that the remains stay with the university for the time being. Before the Bloodkin became involved, several research projects were started. Very little is known about dragon shifters, and the significance of finding any shifter remains that date this far back is more valuable to the historical record than I can say."

Dr. Buckley's historical record thus far was worthless. "When will a determination be made?" Thane asked.

Dr. Buckley frowned. "I really wish you'd consider—"

"When?"

Dr. Buckley sighed heavily. "The infant's DNA was too decayed to test, but we've extracted a few of the female's teeth and are hopeful we can find some intact there. Although, as *she's* apparently not a direct ancestor of yours, it will be the Heolstor mitochondria that we'll be attempting to match. Should be just a few days. No more than a week."

If there was no match, then Thane's claim would prevail. That he had to endure this charade was offensive in the extreme. Heolstor would pay.

Dr. Buckley leaned slightly across the table, as if begging. "I want you to know that I deeply respect the connection, regardless of how distant the kin, that a family has to its forebears. We would treat, and have treated, the female and infant with tremendous care and consideration."

"No," Thane said, failing to swallow the growl that followed the word up his throat.

A muscle in Dr. Buckley's cheek twitched.

Thane sought the finality and release of her death that was long ago robbed from him, but he was met by the guilt that he'd ever doubted her. He braced himself to look at the remains again. "She's not *distant kin*. She was my wife." He then regarded the tray with the darkened bones of the infant, found himself reaching out to touch the skull. "And he was my son."

* * *

EMERSON CLARK PAUSED IN front of the massive doors to the Empire Suite at the Santa Barbara Randolph Hotel.

She smoothed her skirt at the waist and checked the tuck of her silk blouse, finding her clothes none the worse for the few hours of travel from her office in Seattle to Santa Barbara, where the university leading the Kingman Hills project was located. First class was definitely the way to go. Too bad the job took such a toll on the rest of her life.

She leaned forward, rang the bell—*a hotel room with its own doorbell?*—and had a polite smile at the ready.

Do your job. Give notice after.

A man answered the door, casual in jeans and a T-shirt—the quality of the clothes suggested they cost a small fortune. He was tall and fit, with a dazzling smile spreading across his face, making his blue eyes twinkle. Early twenties? The younger son, she guessed. Locke Heolstor.

His forehead creased in confusion. "Can I help you?"

She held out her hand for a shake. "The Heolstor family is expecting me." She'd practiced the pronunciation of the name in the limo on the way over. *He-ol-stor.* "I'm Emerson Clark, the mediator requested to negotiate the Bloodkin claim on the Kingman Hills remains."

"*You're* the mediator? Emerson Clark?"

She smiled. "That's me."

He held up an index finger. "Can you hold on a minute?"

When she nodded, he shut the door again, not quite in her face, but close enough. She pursed her lips and waited. She was paid very well to take such treatment, and Locke had the perfectly highlighted hair and tanned skin of someone who could afford the fee.

She'd just checked her watch—now three minutes past the hour—when the door opened again.

A different man this time, but just as good-looking. Eyes and hair a shade darker, build just as promising, snugged into a perfectly tailored gray suit. She pegged him for the older brother, Ransom.

"Emerson Clark," she repeated. "I'm here for the Heolstor family."

"You are Bloodkin?"

"That's what they tell me." Just as long as they didn't ask her to prove it. *Because dragon shifters? Really?*

He stared.

"Would you like to see some identification?" She pulled her briefcase around and lifted the flap. Maybe then he'd invite her in.

"Emerson," he said.

She glanced up. "Family name."

"Indeed." He touched her arm, stopping her scrounging. "That's really not necessary. I was just taken aback."

"By what?" Dropping her wallet back inside, she closed her briefcase again.

He opened the door wide and gestured for her to enter. "I thought I knew all the Bloodkin." He inclined his head. "All the Bloodkin women, that is."

That right there. That's why she was quitting. The money was not worth the utterly cultish control the Bloodkin had over the members of their community. It was either *in*—with all the luxury she could ever desire—or *out*—with a life of her own. At least she hoped there was an out.

She stepped into a gleaming atrium, a chandelier of crystal and gold overhead. "Well, I'm here now. Shall we begin?"

"Absolutely," he said, though questions still lurked in his eyes.

He'd just have to deal.

The sitting room of the suite—elegant in ivory, pale blue, and gold—was larger than her childhood home. Sunlight diffused to a warm, calming glow through the tall windows that flanked the far side of the room, and an oversized fireplace hulked at the center of the wall, a large bouquet of white blooms on the hearth.

But it was the seductive aroma of coffee that caught her attention.

Please, pretty please, offer me some.

She flicked a glance at the younger brother, who was on the phone. "I see. Yes. Thank you." He gave his older brother a short nod and hung up.

Checking up on me?

Big brother gestured to the tufted white sofa, which turned out to be hard to sit on.

"My apologies, Ms. Clark. I'm Ransom. And this is Locke."

"Pleased to meet you both." She set her briefcase on the floor next to her feet.

"Everyone knows everyone in the Blood," Locke said. "Where have you been hiding?"

Emerson sat up a little straighter. "Not hiding. I'm here, aren't I?"

She hadn't known she was so-called Bloodkin—the term applied to all dragon shifters—until a few years ago, and even now she was certain there'd been a mistake. But she had happily—gratefully—taken Bloodkin funds for school tuition, thinking she'd hit the jackpot. And this job had been waiting for her when she'd graduated, offering her a salary she'd been embarrassed to compare with others from her graduating class. It'd seemed too good to be true…and it was.

"Can I ask about your family?" Locke sat down across from her. "What is your bloodline?"

It was none of their business. "Convoluted."

Consternation tensed Ransom's brow.

Still no offer of coffee. *Okay. Might as well jump in.*

"I've been working with the Kingman Hills project," she said. "I think they're being extra cooperative because they should've informed the Bloodkin immediately that they'd found a possible dragon shifter." *Probably someone who'd had scoliosis.* "I've lodged complaints with both the university and the companies that donated the funds for the research, stating that due to their waiting four months to notify us, the site was paved over for the new shopping center, which impacts our own investigation. Any data, photographs, and samples they've taken of the remains will have to be turned over to us, in their entirety, right away."

Ransom sat down next to his brother. "That sounds excellent."

She nodded. "I'll be repeating the same to Thane Ealdian when I meet with him while you speak with Dr. Buckley at the university."

The brothers exchanged glances.

"Is there a problem?" *Please say no.*

"Have you ever met Mr. Ealdian?" Ransom asked.

She blinked at him. "No. Not yet. Is there something I should know?"

Ransom opened his hands. "You might wonder why we requested mediation in the first place when the law is so clearly on our side…"

"I thought you might be anticipating trouble from the university as they've initiated several research projects since the discovery. I'm taking steps to ensure the research team's full cooperation with regards to the return of the remains." A female in her twenties, with marked deformities, and an infant, who'd been burned. They'd been dug up only to be buried again. She actually kind of felt for Dr. Buckley, who'd seemed devastated at the prospect of losing the remains.

Locke turned his head to his brother in a silent question.

Ransom glanced at him, nodded, then sighed and narrowed his eyes at Emerson as if he were searching for the right words. "We're more concerned about trouble from Thane Ealdian."

Emerson raised her eyebrows. "What kind of trouble?"

"He's been known to be very difficult."

"Will he contest the findings?" The female had been found with the Heolstor sigil, and the family had claimed her. DNA should solve this neatly.

Then she could quit.

"He'll do something," Locke mumbled under his breath.

Emerson cocked her head. "What can he possibly do? Unless the remains are *not* Heolstor? In which case, I'm sure you'll give up your claim."

Please don't draw this out on me.

The brothers were silent. They weren't telling her something. Her hopes were sinking like a two-day-old helium balloon. *Well, crap.*

Locke scooted forward on his seat. "I'd like to accompany you when you meet with Thane."

Emerson smiled slightly. "That really won't be necessary." And it wasn't appropriate.

"He can be very aggressive," Ransom said.

"So can I," she answered.

"He has a reputation for treating women badly."

She smiled broader. "He does so with me, and he'll have hell to pay."

Locke seemed like he was holding his breath.

She scooted forward, too. In order to leave. "Any other questions?"

Locke scratched his head and went all golly-shucks, which didn't seem like his thing at all. "I have one."

"Sure, go ahead."

"I'm wondering if I have to wait until this Kingman Hills business is over before I can ask you out."

Ransom turned his head to glare at his brother as heat flooded her face. "I'm very flattered, of course," she said, "but I'm already in a relationship." Which was a lie, but she was not going to entertain the idea of dating anyone from a Bloodkin family. *Nope. Nuh-uh. No way.* But they sure were nice to look at. This one was a little young for her anyway.

"Lucky guy," Locke said.

Emerson stood, as did the brothers. "If you have any concerns about the remains following your meeting with

Dr. Buckley, please don't hesitate to call me. I'll contact you as soon as the results are in. I'm sure everything will work out just fine."

A girl can hope.

"We'll do that," Ransom said as he walked her to the door. "My father wasn't able to fly in, but I know that this dispute weighs heavily on his mind. Finding lost kin and having its identity in question has been intolerable for him. And communication with Thane Ealdian has been…less than civil."

That would be Gerard Heolstor, patriarch, philanthropist, and statesman before his retirement.

Maybe the whole dragon thing was metaphorical? Fierce negotiators, or ruthless in the boardroom. Maybe it was hype. And then at some point, maybe when the other shifter clans were organizing politically, the so-called dragons jumped on the bandwagon. There was a big difference, however, between a person shifting into an animal that actually existed—like a wolf, bear, or panther—and one that was entirely mythological.

The remains of one deformed woman did not and could not confirm the existence of dragons, no matter what Dr. Buckley hypothesized. And Emerson very much doubted that the Heolstor brothers could prove anything, either. She certainly didn't have a dragon lurking inside of her. Well, maybe without coffee.

With a hand to her shoulder, Ransom kept her from

exiting. "Could I trouble you to visit us at our family home while we await the results? Hearing first-hand what steps you've taken might settle my father somewhat."

Emerson fought back a sigh. She was supposed to be at their disposal for the duration of the mediation. She just hadn't considered that she would be settling a dispute between the families themselves, rather than merely between the families and the university.

"I'd be happy to meet with your father," she said, though she had a feeling this was less about the old man and more about getting the edge on Thane Ealdian. "You have my contact information. Just let me know when is convenient for him."

She held out her hand for a good-bye shake, but Ransom took it and held it. "If not one of us, will you please consider taking someone with you to meet with Mr. Ealdian?"

She nodded. "I'll do that." Consider it, that is.

The door was just closing behind her when she overheard Locke tell Ransom, "Good thinking. Keep her away from Thane."

Dragons? She'd worked for them for a year, kept her eyes and ears open, and she still didn't believe it for a minute.

CHAPTER 2

"THEY SENT A *MEDIATOR* to deal with me?" Thane was trembling on the verge of change. Again. He'd suffered through the meeting with Dr. Buckley, and gazing upon the remains of his wife and boy, his heir, had been difficult enough, but this? This was an outrage.

He could almost feel his son, warm and pink with life, in his hands. Smell that sweet milky scent. Gaze upon the deep blue of his eyes, so wide and alert that Thane knew he'd have grown up strong. Been a leader, heir to the Ealdian hoard. The finest black dragon…ever.

Did the Heolstors think he was so far gone that he wouldn't fight to bring his family home at last? They deserved to come home. To be put to rest. Honored.

"Yes, sir. A Bloodkin by the name of Emerson Clark." Matthew had been with him for centuries, sustained by dragon blood, but this past decade into Thane's sixty-year seclusion, he'd taken to standing across the room when delivering news of any kind.

"Clark isn't a Blood name," Thane observed. But Emerson was. Or had been once. In fact, he remembered a time long, long ago when it had been Emmerich.

"Shall I take the meeting on your behalf?"

The Heolstor claim was an insult, a prevarication, a ploy. They knew very well that their family tree was complete, the bones of all their dead gone to ash. That Carreen had gripped their sigil through the ages didn't mean she belonged to them. She'd held it all that time so that she could hand it to her husband. A gift, like the peace of an olive branch—the identity of their child's murderer.

It meant she hadn't run away after all. The rumors that Thane himself had been responsible for the deaths of his wife and their son would finally be put to rest, too.

"No," Thane said. Matthew had taken on the Ealdian business affairs in preparation for Thane's final shift into his dragon, but Thane would handle this himself, as a man. He wouldn't dishonor Carreen's act of courage by returning his ear to the Night Song, no matter how sweetly it called him into fire and flight. "Send the mediator to me when he comes."

"What are you going to do?"

Matthew knew him so well.

Thane would handle this the old way. "I'm going to eat him."

* * *

"MY MEETINGS SHOULD BE done by five at the latest," Emerson said to her long-ago foster brother Bryan as she exited the limousine. *Bryan! I get to see Bryan!* Was it professional to dance in the street? "Then I'll head over." Bryan and Mexican food—the perfect combo.

"I'll be there," he said. "Can't wait to see you, Ember."

Emerson grinned. Ember. She'd thought the name was so cool when she was seventeen. "Feeling's mutual. You have no idea."

Bryan was the closest thing she had to a brother. She should've kept in better touch. The Bloodkin controlled so much of her life, but they didn't control her phone.

Tip in hand, she leaned down to the front passenger window of the limo to speak to the driver.

"Thank you so much for your help today. I don't think I'll need you anymore." She was already downtown, and the restaurant wasn't far.

"Please, no," he said, warding off the cash. "It's

already taken care of."

Of course it was.

She stepped back onto the sidewalk, inhaling deeply, enjoying the early summer afternoon air. So far, everything about Santa Barbara was gorgeous—the weather, the flowers in bloom, the hope for new life. Maybe she'd move here after she quit.

Then she marched up the steps of the townhouse in front of her. Mr. Ealdian had apparently taken an entire home instead of putting himself up in a hotel for a few days while he met with Dr. Buckley at the university. A whole house. Who did that?

For the second time that day, she rang a doorbell. Waiting, she smoothed her skirt and patted her blouse. With any luck, she'd be done here in half an hour.

The door opened to a man in a trim navy suit, slightly balding, with sea-gray eyes. His composure was so quiet and contained that she concluded he must be Matthew Chandler, Mr. Ealdian's personal secretary, with whom she'd been corresponding by e-mail.

She held out her hand. "Emerson Clark for Mr. Ealdian."

Pink spots flushed the man's cheeks. Then, clearly unsettled, he stepped aside, gaze dropping to the gleaming hardwood floors. "Please...*my lady*, do come in."

Again, expecting a guy. What was the Bloodkin's

problem with women who had androgynous names? It's not like Emerson was *that* uncommon for a girl. "You seem surprised."

"Begging your pardon," he said, deeply apologetic. "Your name contains a patronymic. Emer*son*. I made a foolish assumption."

"Please don't worry about it." She entered, taking in the tall foyer, spare but spacious, with a long console to the right and a sweeping stair to the left in the same deep, gleaming wood as the floor. Very elegant. Very money.

"Are you accompanied?" Mr. Chandler stood at the threshold, searching the street. The limo had already pulled away.

"No, it's just me today."

He stepped back inside. "My apologies again, but I'm afraid I will have to reschedule your appointment."

Because of her *name*? She stared at him, and then reminded herself that she was going to quit. Maybe even this week if the university continued to cooperate.

"All right. Would you like to set another appointment now," she asked, "or would you like to consult with Mr. Ealdian and contact me later?"

"I will contact you shortly."

"That will be fine. It was nice meeting you." *Or not meeting you.*

She turned and reached for the door handle to let herself out, but he put a hand to the door.

"Of course, I'll have a car take you." Mr. Chandler sounded appalled at the thought of her leaving alone.

"No, thank you. It's a lovely day. I'd like to walk."

"A Bloodkin woman *does not*—"

"I'll be fine." *Because* this *Bloodkin woman does.*

He moved—or avoided touching her—and she wrenched the door open. The likelihood of crime in this neighborhood was nil, and now she could meet with Bryan even earlier. At last, she had an evening on her terms. What a concept.

She was on the stoop when Mr. Chandler spoke behind her. "My lord, please stay where you are."

Because women are so dangerous?

"Is Emerson Clark here?" a low voice rumbled.

Emerson hung her head. *So close.*

"There's been a mistake," Mr. Chandler said.

"Why do I scent a woman?"

Emerson huffed silently. *Scent? Must be her girl cooties.*

She sighed. *Might as well get this over with.*

She pasted on an extra sunny smile and turned back toward the house. "Mr. Ealdian?" She remained on the stoop but leaned to the side to address the shadow on the stairs. "I'm happy to reschedule for whatever time suits. It's really no problem."

A man descended the last few stairs and came into the light. *Oh, sweet Lord.* Did all the Bloodkin have such excellent genes? Thane Ryce Ealdian was way younger than she expected. Mid-thirties, maybe. Sandy hair. Less dashing than the Heolstor brothers, but his cut jaw, full mouth, and the line of his brow were blunt in their sensuality. He was tall and lean, those muscles no doubt developed with the help of a personal trainer and chef. Her belly fluttered in response—*this* Bloodkin, so…raw, was much more her type.

When he stepped fully into the sunlight, she attempted to cover a snort of laughter with a cough and ended up with watery eyes and wheezy breathing instead. He was wearing deep indigo contact lenses with a vertical slit for the pupil. Maybe not her type, after all.

"Please, excuse me." She fanned her face and blinked back tears. "Allergies."

This was so rude. She was a professional. Up till now, she'd prided herself on her composure. Clearly, this guy was really into the dragon shifter thing, and she respected that, but man, he'd just taken her by surprise.

"You've met with the Heolstor family?" He did have a wonderful voice, so low and resonant that she could feel it in her chest like the bass guitar in a club. "What did Gerard say?"

"Actually, I met with his sons." She held out her hand. "By the way, I'm Emerson Clark. I'll be handling the mediation for the Kingman Hills project."

His hand was dry and hot and strong. "You mean the mediation between Gerard and me?"

She smiled with a shallow nod. "I'm picking up on that, yes."

Finally, someone who could be direct. She could be, too. "I'm also coming to understand that my being a woman presents a problem."

"I planned on eating the man Emerson Clark alive."

She laughed out loud.

He merely lifted a brow. "Are you coming inside?"

Her gaze went to Mr. Chandler, who'd basically just kicked her out. He was pale and his expression crestfallen. He gave a subtle, pleading shake of his head. *No.*

So silly. She wasn't going to tell on him.

She looked back into Mr. Ealdian's very interesting contact lenses. "If I could have just a few minutes of your time to bring you up to speed?"

He gracefully pivoted to clear the doorway, saying silkily, "After you."

* * *

SENDING A WOMAN WAS *not* a mistake. Whatever momentary confusion her name had caused, someone had arranged it. No question.

Thane guided her to the house's study, a hand just skimming the back of her silk blouse. "Can I get you something to drink?"

He stopped at the bar cart to pour himself a glass of Scotch. He needed to give himself something to do. Strangers unsettled him, pumping his blood just a little too fast to be completely safe. And a woman... Well, he'd not allowed one close for years now.

She walked deeper into the study, standing in the center of the room just before the overlarge desk. One of her arms touched the briefcase hanging near her hip. Not quite nervous. As Bloodkin, she should know to be at the very least wary of an old dragon. *We bite.*

She was shorter than most dragon-born. She had clear brown eyes that were level and circumspect. Her light brown hair was too straight to be natural, a layer cut to frame her face. She had a pouty mouth, merely glossed. Her narrow skirt fell to the knee. And her blouse barely showed the notch between her collarbones. She was curvy, but she wasn't here to seduce. Nevertheless, his fingertips itched to touch her. All of her.

What did they mean by throwing a Bloodkin woman at a dragon near his change? A distraction? A peace offering? For his *wife and child?* No.

"The Heolstor brothers seemed just as surprised when they met me," she said.

"Were they?" He held up his Scotch to remind her of his offer.

"Oh, no, thank you," she said as she looked around the study. It wasn't his, so she'd learn nothing if she were here to spy.

"How did your meeting with Dr. Buckley go?" she asked.

"The remains of the woman and child belong to me." He'd only allow this farce to play so long, abiding by the Bloodkin Assembly's strictures on inter-kin conflicts. In this modern age, the Triad who controlled the Assembly had become absolute on maintaining secrecy about dragon matters. No fighting. No fire in the sky. "And the Heolstors know it, too."

"I wouldn't be surprised," she said and returned her direct gaze to him. "Nevertheless, there is a process."

How politic. She seemed too intelligent to allow herself to be a pawn.

She went on to describe the actions she'd taken with the university and the donors. When he requested documentation, she reached into her briefcase and produced it. Efficient. Prepared. If she *was* a pawn, she wasn't a helpless one.

"I hope you can understand," he said, "how offensive this process is when the remains being kept from me are that of my late wife and son."

The space between her brows wrinkled in what seemed like momentary confusion. Thoughts flickered behind her eyes—*she hadn't known about his loss?*—but she kept her composure. "I will do my utmost to bring it to a speedy—"

Thane slapped the desk in frustration and felt one of its legs give with a crash. "Who sent you?"

She blinked at the noise, startled, but she didn't shrink. "My boss informed me that a Bloodkin had to handle this matter, and so here I am."

"Who? *A name*. Who directed you to take on this mediation?" Her involvement had to have somehow been arranged by the Heolstors. *Have this woman for the one we took from you.* He was not so easily bought.

A knock sounded at the door.

Thane ignored it.

The door opened anyway.

"My lord, if I may—"

Thane inclined his head over his shoulder, snarling. "Get out."

When he looked back at Emerson Clark, her gaze was full of censure, but still no fear. If anything, she was showing more grit. "My boss is Martin Fraser."

Thane was not so unaffected. "Fraser isn't a Bloodkin name."

"I'm not sure who's Bloodkin and who's not within the company. I just do my work as well as I can."

Not sure who...? Unbelievable.

Of course, the Bloodkin had staff all over the world—lawyers and businessmen to manage concerns. Few were kin themselves, and those who were of the Blood, were young like this Emerson—*a ridiculous name for a woman*—

and only there to educate themselves on how the world's networks operated.

"Were you taught nothing as a child?" he spat.

The muscles in her clenched jaw twitched. Her eyes challenged him.

Fire and burn, how she got his blood up. Her scent was affecting him, too. All those modern products loaded with perfumes. He passed a knuckle over his mouth to breathe through it.

Her gaze dropped to his hand and lingered on his fingertips for a moment. These past years, the dragon growing emergent, his nails had grown black, thick, and slightly tapered.

She rolled her eyes.

Shock warred with a flare of his anger.

"I think I saw a fly." She stepped back, putting space between them and exaggerating her movements as she looked around the room.

He couldn't help himself. He laughed. What a little liar. Thane Ryce Ealdian had stalked this earth for over a thousand years, and she thought him a fool. Thought the signs of his imminent final shift were…what? An affectation?

"Are you Bloodkin or not?" he demanded.

"I am."

"Are you sure?" She didn't sound it and seemed utterly ignorant of their ways.

She swallowed hard and took a deep breath. "I apologize deeply for any offense I might have caused."

He'd bet gold she was going to blame her "allergies" again.

"Really, the pollen is killing my eyes," she said. "I'd better go."

Ha!

She made a wide berth around him to get to the door. "Mr. Chandler has my contact information if you need me. And I'll be in touch when I hear from Dr. Buckley."

"Stay," he commanded.

She opened the study door. "I'm sorry, I can't. I have a dinner date."

"With whom? One of the Heolstors? Ransom or Locke?"

She smiled politely. "No, neither. Rest assured, this has nothing to do with the Bloodkin."

And then she had the gall to turn her back on him and start down the hallway to the front door.

The dragon stretched within him. His vision went hazy, breath hot. His gaze lingered on her tiny waist and the sway of her rounded hips.

"My lord—" Matthew clutched the hilt of his short sword, sheathed at his belt under his suit jacket. Did he think to use it on his lord to save *her*? Had the whole world gone mad?

"I'll be in touch." Emerson Clark opened the door

and walked out.

A Bloodkin woman of age, with no protection but her intelligent eyes and that clever mouth.

Thane gaped after her. "What is she?"

Matthew shook his head. "I don't know. Bait? Or a provocation?"

Meant to force his final shift into dragon? Thane growled. "The first casualty, more like."

"My lord?"

Thane turned away from the sunlight, disgusted. "In what will most certainly become a war. Follow her. See that she gets wherever she's going safely."

CHAPTER 3

EMERSON STOOD AT THE restaurant's bar, her skin hot with anger, frustration, and that omnipresent prickle of fear. Apparently, it didn't matter what city she was in, the Bloodkin always had someone following her.

The restaurant bar was packed with people drinking margaritas and noshing on tortilla chips. The place was vibrant with color—reds, oranges, yellows, and greens— and the decibel level of music and chatter hovered at ear ringing. She found it comforting, concealing.

She wished Bryan would get there. Get his take on the Bloodkin situation. She'd lived with it alone for too long, and no one else she'd complained or reported it to had done anything to change it.

Leaning down to eat a salsa-laden tortilla chip, she cut a surreptitious glance to her left, where, yes, Mr. Chandler was discreetly watching her. He was a nondescript, near-invisible suit against the far wall. He wasn't trying to hide from her—more like pretending to be secret service—which didn't make it any better.

She was tempted to approach him and demand that he leave, but she'd tried that in the past with others and they'd just moved to watch her from another spot. What really burned was that she didn't know when it had begun. At first, she'd only been suspicious, that niggling feeling on the back of her neck. And when she'd become certain—about six months ago—her boss explained that all the Bloodkin in the office had been assigned security because of problems with an ex-employee. And she'd accepted that until she noticed that almost everything in her life was owned or controlled by the Bloodkin.

The restaurant door opened and a man with a familiar, though older, face entered, his gaze searching the crowd.

"Bry!" Emerson went up on tiptoes to wave, her spirits rising. Everything was going to be okay now.

He weaved through the crowd toward her, and she couldn't help smiling and bouncing in anticipation. He'd grown up good. Tall and lanky. His hair was scruffy and too long, but it suited him. And those brown eyes had always been so warm.

When he hugged her, he lifted her off her feet, exactly what she needed after today. He pecked her quickly on the mouth before setting her down. "Ember, you have no idea how good it is to see you."

"Well, if I was coming to Santa Barbara, I was going to see you." She rubbed her thumb on his chin stubble. She remembered when his scruff had been patchy at best. "You look great! I want to hear everything."

She couldn't believe it had been seven years. Her family was a bunch of foster kids whose fates had aligned with hers at some point before glancing off in other directions, and now she was determined to get them back in her life.

"Me, too." He stepped back, glancing up and down in an obvious appraisal of her outfit. "You look fancy."

She forced herself not to glance over at Mr. Chandler. "I've been in meetings all day."

"Big deal in the works?"

"Mediation. Making people play nicely with each other." She gave him a wry quirk of her eyebrows. "I'm a very expensive babysitter." And if Mr. Chandler was eavesdropping, he was welcome to pass that along to Mr. Ealdian.

"So, it pays well?"

She hadn't meant to sound like she was bragging. "Not for long." She lowered her voice. "I'm quitting."

"Oh, yeah? When?"

"Soon. A week at most. As soon as this is done. I want to go out on a positive note."

The pager in her hand buzzed, red lights blinking all over it. The wait for a table was going on an hour, so it'd been good that she'd arrived early. She grinned. "We're up."

They were seated at a comparatively quiet table away from the bar. She could no longer see Mr. Chandler, but she was sure he was there somewhere.

The chips, salsa, and guac were all done by the time Bryan related the basics in his life. He'd been dating, but no one special. His pack was okay, but he and the Alpha didn't see eye to eye, so he might go lone wolf. Bryan had always known he was Wolfkin. His wolf had just started to manifest when he and Emerson were put in the same home together, his previous foster mom having tried to beat the animal out of him. A beaten dog just gets more feral.

Then it was her turn. Emerson wasn't seeing anyone *at all*. Her hours just didn't allow for it. She didn't tell Bryan that she knew if she *did* meet someone, the guy would just turn out to be Bloodkin. Some shiny pretty boy, like Locke. Or sexy Thane, with his weirdo contact lenses. Basically, her life was work, work, work.

"Would've never guessed that you'd go into business," Bryan said as their entrées arrived. She'd gone with the cheesy enchilada in celebration of hanging with him, but truth be told, Bryan's sizzling and snapping steak fajitas looked pretty damn good.

He picked up a warm tortilla. "So your job is making you unhappy?"

Here goes. She'd been waiting for an opening, and now she was nervous.

"It's more the office environment. The people. The life." If she could talk to anyone about the creepiness of being Bloodkin, it was Bryan. Of course, *he* could actually shift into a wolf so their situations weren't exactly the same. But he had his pack, and she had the company. "It's kind of odd."

He lifted his brows in question while he took a man bite of his stuffed tortilla.

"Well, the company exclusively serves the Bloodkin," she said.

He choked and grabbed for his water.

Not a good sign. But, yeah, her thoughts exactly.

She glanced over her shoulder to see if Mr. Chandler was near. No sign of him.

"No kidding, they pay well," Bryan said when he recovered. "You must've been a star student to get recruited by them. Smarty-pants."

She winced. "I worked hard in school, but I think my being there has more to do with long-lost family ties than anything."

Bryan's forehead wrinkled.

Emerson sighed. "As in, supposedly, I'm Bloodkin, too."

She took a sip of her margarita while he stared at her. He finally wiped his mouth, the look of confusion still troubling his expression. "So I'm dining with royalty, eh?"

"Don't tease me. The people are so…" *Crazy.* Thane Ealdian thought the six-hundred-year-old skeletons were his dead wife and kid.

"And you're going to quit?"

"Yes. Reminding myself gets me through every day. I just don't understand them." The Bloodkin had taken over all facets of her life down to the gym she went to and when. She lived in an apartment building they owned. They followed her, paid for things, beat up a guy who'd tried to hit on her. Hell, the seat next to her in first class had been empty on her "full" flight.

Bryan picked up his food again. "Well, they're dragons."

"Some are," she said.

"Apparently *you* are. Have you shifted?"

"Pfft, no. No shifting. I might be Bloodkin, but I'm no dragon. I'm distantly *related* to someone who thought he was. I'd know if I were a dragon, wouldn't I? In fact, I've seen no dragons at all. Not even a suggestion that dragons are *real.*" Mr. Ealdian's contact lenses and claws

didn't count. "These are very wealthy, very eccentric people. And if you repeat that, I'll probably be fired. So I guess I should thank you."

"I wouldn't dare repeat it," Bryan said. "My Alpha would beat me senseless."

"What?"

"Pack life. Forget it. The Bloodkin are very powerful, and supposedly, they have very long memories when it comes to who crosses them. So leave on good terms…if you *can* leave that is. I've never heard of a lone dragon."

"I was a lone dragon most of my life."

"Won the foster-kid lottery, though."

She laughed. "I thought that, too, at first." Not so much now. "They always have someone following me." She leaned forward. "Even tonight. Here."

"They have the best security in the world," Bryan said. "Some wolves I know have worked for them."

He didn't seem to get it.

"But I didn't hire security," she said. "And I don't want it. I just want to live my life like any other normal person. But they are everywhere."

He put down his second tortilla. "Has anyone hurt you or threatened you? Inhibited your movements?"

"No. They mostly anticipate my movements and then I just end up doing what they want me to. I feel trapped, controlled." Her eyes burned, so she picked up her drink and took a sip. She'd thought Bryan would understand.

"They protect their own."

"Taking over my life is *protection*?" She shook her head. "You're as crazy as they are."

"No, I'm *kin*. Shifter life in a pack is very different from mainstream human life—archaic, bonded, rigid— and we wolves are not the stuff of legend. Shifter life among the magical elite is bound to be another world altogether."

She sighed. "I don't want it. I want out. I was hoping you'd help me."

"You don't know what you're asking." He lifted his tortilla and took a bite.

Emerson forced a smile to cover her hurt. "I understand. I'll figure it out."

She wasn't about to lose him now that they'd reconnected. She'd caught him off guard, and obviously, he was under constraints with his pack. His pack Alpha sounded awful. Maybe Bryan was just as trapped as she was. Maybe *kin*—Wolf or Blood—meant *cage*.

"Sadie's back in rehab," Bryan said after a moment's silence.

Emerson's strained smile faded, thrown by his abrupt segue. Sadie had been an alcoholic at fourteen, and it had gone downhill from there. For a summer, though, the three of them had been inseparable. One night they'd held on to each other as tightly as they could while ambulance lights repeatedly hit their foster home like lightning. And then they'd been pulled apart.

"How did you find her?" Emerson wondered why she hadn't even looked.

"Sniffed her out this past year. I've been trying to get her into this new treatment place that seems really good. Might help her more than her current program," Bryan said. "Now I'm thinking you're in a position to help me."

"Is that so?" Emerson picked up her fork and tried to focus on Sadie, not the isolation boxing in her heart.

"There's a long waiting list. A call from a Bloodkin could push her to the top."

"I'll see what I can do," Emerson said. At least her Bloodkin status might be good for something. And thanks to Bryan, now she had another sibling within reach. "Send me the information."

After dinner, he wouldn't let her go back to her hotel alone, and he saw her up to her door. Her small suite didn't have the splendor the Heolstor brothers' did, but it was still an upscale apartment. The enormous basket of fruit, chocolate, and champagne—courtesy of the hotel—had to be a Bloodkin perk. And the robe and slippers? A "gift" from management.

She was pretty sure wolf shifters didn't get this kind of treatment. He must think she was so spoiled.

"Thanks for bringing me back," she said. "Want to come in? Hang out?" She was tired but didn't want to let go of him and her old life so soon, even if she did have a flight back to Seattle early in the morning.

"Ah, no, but thanks. And you're welcome." He kissed her on the forehead then sighed heavily. "Been thinking about your situation…"

Her heart double beat, but she didn't want to get her hopes up.

"You're going to have trouble leaving your job. I can't see why the Bloodkin wouldn't let you quit, but they will hold on to you somehow. Before you make any announcements to your boss, maybe test the waters first."

"I can't stay there," she said. "You have no idea."

"I might, actually, but we'll work it out. It's possible you'll need to slip out of your current life and disappear. As in, change your name, the works. We'll need a strategy, though, so until then, tread carefully. We'll find a way." He chuckled. "Bloodkin. Of all things, Ember."

He kept saying *we*.

Her eyes were burning again. She knew he'd be there for her.

She turned to unlock her hotel room door, pushed it partially open, and held it there with her foot. "Send me the info for Sadie," she said. They'd all take care of each other.

Bryan had already started down the hall to the elevators, but he lifted a hand.

It'd been seven years, and she'd missed him. To let

him know, she yipped and howled softly, like old times. Their little vagabond pack.

Bryan didn't turn around, but he threw back his head, opened his arms, and howled from his gut.

* * *

THANE MARVELED AT THE car Matthew had procured for him. The last time he'd driven an automobile had been in the nineteen forties, and it had looked nothing like this. Yesterday, he'd asked for something fast, an automobile worthy of an Ealdian. The Audi R8 before him was a long, sleek bullet, low to the ground, with a grill on the front as if it were baring its teeth. It was black, of course, like an Ealdian dragon, with silver details. The workmanship clearly superb.

"My lord Thane—"

Thane waved Matthew silent. He could transport himself. He *would* transport himself.

Powers were in motion, tactics in play. He couldn't hesitate a moment. Whoever had sent Emerson Clark had already made the first move, and Thane had been so long out of the world he hadn't even known that an Emmerich still lived.

Sixty years had passed while he'd been in self-imposed isolation. The solace had been a necessary balm to the agitation and flashes of fire that had sometimes clouded his mind. He'd missed the power and strength of becoming the dragon—missed it like a parched man missed water, even—but there was a point in every Bloodkin's life when he knew he might not have the will to shift back. He might lose himself to the dragon.

He'd already lived longer than most. The dragon within could be denied only so long, and then it would claim his mind and force its way to the surface. He had to be on Havyn, the isle where old dragons went to fly and flame and fall to ash, when that occurred, or as with dragons in eons past, he might ravage the land and bring the condemnation and violence of humanity down upon the Bloodkin. Dragons would be hunted again.

But Matthew's present concern about his state of mind was unwarranted. Thane would not shift today, nor at all until this business was complete. And he could not allow himself to be chauffeured from place to place, either. His allies would doubt him. He was old, not helpless.

Besides, a car like this promised a singularly pleasurable experience.

"Does it fly?" Because that might be a problem.

Matthew sighed. "No, my lord."

Thane smiled. Then he'd just have to figure the thing out.

"Do you have a map?" he asked Matthew. It was some distance to his destination.

The day was bright and crisp, a sweet cacophony of sensation bombarding him. A deep breath, and energy sang through his veins. His dragon reveled in response. All this, it wanted. All this and more.

"I've already given the car the address," Matthew said. "You need only follow its instructions where to turn and so forth."

"You sound frightened." Usually, Matthew kept all traces of dread out of his voice.

"My lord Thane, I am terrified."

* * *

THE ORVYN STRONGHOLD WAS nestled in a remote corner of the Sierra Nevada Mountains, surrounded by sequoias that had scraped the sky longer than any dragon had. Standing on the cobble stoned circular driveway in front of the entrance, Thane ignored the alpine sentries and frowned at the long scratches on the side of the automobile.

A three hour drive, and he was grieved that he'd damaged the thing. He'd come to love it in such a short time. The car's power was not only located in the engine; it seemed to permeate the entire vehicle. Somewhere there was a human engineer who dreamed of flying like a dragon, and he'd gotten very close with this car.

A Bloodkin came to stand beside him and also

surveyed the damage. From her scent alone, he knew her. Lena Orvyn, Carreen's sister.

"Did you kill anyone driving?" Her melodic voice was the same, too.

"Not yet," he said, turning toward her. "Though Matthew may be dead from excessive worry."

Lena wore the passage of time well. Her russet hair curled over her shoulder, and her gold eyes still sparked. She'd never used cosmetics, and except for a slight pallor today, had never required any, either. Her pants were long, but he guessed she was wearing high heels because she was taller than he remembered.

He took her hands in his. "Have you been to see them?"

Lena was the only one who'd be just as devastated as he was at the discovery of Carreen's and Rinc's remains. Together, they'd searched, followed every rumor, but their efforts had come to nothing.

"I will when the mediation is settled, when I can take my time to say my farewells." She sounded tired. Six hundred years' worth of uncertainty. "After so long, what's a few more days?"

"She was holding the Heolstor sigil."

She cocked her head slightly in rebuke. "Anyone could've put it there."

"I was in a dispute with Gerard at the time."

"And he's always had a temper, I know." She touched

his arm to turn him toward the house. "Come inside, and I'll tell you what I've discovered about your mediator."

"Then you agree that her sudden appearance means something?" He'd called Lena immediately upon Emerson Clark's departure for her "dinner date." Matthew hadn't been able to hear anything she and her man had said over the din of the restaurant, but he had managed to take a photograph on his mobile, the small device that had rarely left Matthew's person these past few years.

"Honestly, I don't know what to think," Lena said.

Thane didn't like going indoors—his dragon balked at small spaces—but Lena was a dragon as well, so her entryway was vast, clean, and cold. She brought him down a short step and to the left into a large room of soothing grays with roomy leather benches for furniture. She kept her treasure hidden, but somewhere here in her lair, there was plenty of it. A dragon didn't advertise.

"Do you know who controls her?" he asked. Lena had ties to Godric Tredan, one of the Triad that governed the Bloodkin Assembly and, therefore, a source of unadulterated information.

"No. There's nothing like that. No Blood family at all, which is simply shocking. Somehow, as a child, Emerson ended up in the *human* social services. Her tie to the Bloodkin was evidently not discovered until she applied for financial aid for university."

There were many things wrong with Lena's narration, but he started with the obvious. "Financial aid."

"That bothered me, too."

A dragon without means. Unheard of.

Lena produced a piece of paper—the financial aid form, it seemed. Page five asked the applicant if he or she were full or part shifter. Emerson had the yes box checked, and on the line provided to note the kind of shifter, she'd written—scrawled, more like—*dragon* with a question mark. The Bloodkin would've confirmed it once notified, so there was no question any longer.

"Where is the rest of this form?"

She handed him a folder. "It has to be a fabrication."

Thane paged through the sheaf. Emerson's middle name was Adele. *Much* better. Her address at the time had been in Reno—he'd have to check that—and she was young, just twenty-five, according to the birthdate on the form. A dragon's age was always hard to determine on sight. "Parents deceased."

"They didn't find their rest on Havyn," Lena said. "They must have met human deaths."

"Yet they named her Emerson," he said. It was her name that bothered him the most.

"Just so."

"And then kept her existence secret from the Bloodkin?" *Give her a dragon family name, but deny her contact with others of her kind?* "And yet she *knew* her origins or she

45

wouldn't have made herself known for this absurd financial aid."

There *had been* that question mark next to her shifter designation. Maybe Emerson hadn't known for sure.

"What did you think of her?" Lena asked.

Thane recalled his impressions of Emerson Clark. "Direct. Capable." Puzzling. She'd laughed at him. "Fearless."

"Then a potential enemy?"

No, Emerson was… "She seemed to have the recklessness of youth. She's smart, but not suspicious."

Lena's brows went up. "You liked her."

"She was there and gone before I had a chance to come to any conclusions, but Matthew was ready to defend her after one minute."

"Pretty?"

Thane narrowed his eyes. "I *have* considered that she was sent as a bribe."

Lena nodded her head. "This Emerson for Carreen. And Emerson could bear an Ealdian heir."

Thane shook his head. "I don't think she has the guile to persuade in that way. Not knowingly. Not yet." Though it would be amusing—no, *interesting*—to watch her attempt to seduce. "And remember, I told you she said she had a dinner date. What of him?"

As if on cue, Lena opened another file and handed him a large page with the photograph of Emerson at dinner with the young man, the same picture that Matthew had shown him on his device last night. In the photo, Emerson's smile lit her eyes, her complexion flushed with joy. She'd leaned in to hear what her equally avid partner was saying.

"Bryan Rand, Wolfkin. He escorted her back to her hotel room."

A wolf of all things. "You see?" Thane waved at the photo. "Everything about her is nonsensical. A dragon who lies with a wolf? I suppose pigs fly and the moon is blue, too."

"She's a modern woman. She can take a lover before settling on a Blood union."

"Women have taken lovers in every age," Thane cut back.

Lena flinched. "Forgive me. That was clumsy."

Thane waved her apology aside. Carreen had proved her loyalty when she'd attempted to shift in order to protect Rinc. Whatever troubles they'd had between them, she had been the fierce mother he'd wanted for their child.

"Hear me," he said. "Whatever the scheme behind Emerson Clark's sudden appearance, this will come to war." They'd burned his son, disfigured his wife.

Lena gave a little laugh. "The last time you tried to avenge my sister, you scorched hundreds of innocents from the earth. And your dragon wasn't even ascendant then. If the Night Song calls to *me*—and brother, its call is a beautiful and bitter reckoning I haven't the strength to deny much longer—then that same music must be in your very blood now. Just think: another year, and you would've been Thane no longer. You would've been a shadow above the clouds, senseless to anything but the burning stars."

"I will do my duty by Carreen and Rinc."

"So you will, but this age has weapons that can destroy dragons."

"Every age has weapons that can destroy dragons," he told her. "But the old ways were more brutal than anything modern man can conceive."

"Every age is savage, or the Bloodkin wouldn't endure. Our allies are stirring—I have word from Algar and Pearce already—though I doubt you will need them. The news has spread that you've abandoned your seclusion." She lifted her hands dramatically. Only she would dare. "Thane Ealdian prowls the earth once more. Shutter your houses. Bar your doors. Offer him gold and women to satisfy his cravings. A black dragon is like the very devil himself."

He didn't laugh. "Emerson Clark will not assuage my anger." No matter how much he was tempted. "If my enemies think she will, it might be best for me to end the Emmerich line once and for all."

CHAPTER 4

EMERSON HIT SEND ON her e-mail to Bryan regarding the arrangements she'd just made for Sadie. After her flight back to Seattle this morning, a quick stop to freshen up at home and then another to her favorite coffee spot, she'd come in to the office and taken care of it first thing. Family first. It was how she was going to start taking her life back from the Bloodkin.

Happy for the first time in a long time, she ducked out of her office to grab a cookie. Someone had left a platter of homemade chocolate chip on the table in the break room, and the buttery smell had sneaked across the hall, under her nose, and eroded her willpower. She wanted one, and they *were* there for everyone—including, she presumed, the office freak.

The hum of office chatter muted as she stepped out of her door and into the open space containing a small warren of cubicles, around which the individual offices stood. She didn't have to look to know that gazes would be tracking her movements. For pity's sake, her Blood status wasn't contagious.

Over the past year she'd worked for the company, everyone had always been *very* polite to her, but no one had grown friendly. It didn't help that her office was set apart from the others who had started working there around the same time. Spacious and beautifully decorated with modern lines and minimalist color, her office had a wall of windows overlooking the city skyline. Regardless of the weather—blue skies, cloudy, stormy—the view was incredible. And she hadn't earned it. Didn't want it. She would trade the whole thing to be invited to lunch by any of them. *Her* invitations had all been politely turned down. Every last one.

The break room was empty, a large table at its center where she'd once tried eating to put herself in everyone else's traffic pattern, but they'd just stayed away—actually preferred to go hungry—until she'd left.

Grabbing a napkin, she selected a fat cookie. It had that pretty golden goodness to it—gold was her favorite color—and she could tell it was the chewy kind. Chewy chocolate chip cookies were the best. But now that she had it, she was tempted to save it for later. Hoard it for the right moment. The thought made her grin. Maybe she was part dragon, after all.

She walked back into her office and to her desk, and the door shut behind her.

Someone cleared his throat, and she startled, whirling around.

An unfamiliar man in rumpled khakis and a half-untucked pale-blue button-down stood staring at her. He was middle-aged, his hair thinning. He had a slightly crooked nose, red face, and was sweating profusely.

"Can I help you?" she asked.

"The remains found at Kingman Hills belong to the Heolstors," he said quickly, as if by rote.

"I'm sorry, but who are you?" She might've held out her hand, but she was holding her cookie.

"It doesn't matter who I am." He wrung his hands. "I've been sent to help you. If you want to get out of this alive, you will report that the remains belong to the Heolstors."

Get out of this alive? Her heart thumped hard. She moved to her desk phone, dropped her cookie, and hit the button for reception. "If they are Heolstor remains, then that's what I will say."

Teresa picked up right away. "Yes, Ms. Clark?"

"I need security. Immediately." How had he gotten

past their desk on the ground floor anyway?

"Tell *no one*," the man repeated.

"Did the Heolstors send you?" She hated her job. That Ransom had seemed a little shifty.

The man heaved a shaky breath, as if struggling for no apparent reason. "No, a friend sent me."

"I don't like your friends."

"No. This is a friend of *yours*." He lifted the untucked part of his shirt and pulled a black gun from his front right pocket. *"Don't tell anyone."*

Her body flashed cold with terror as she ducked behind the desk for protection, but she kept her gaze on him. "Stop! Please. What do you want? I'll get it for you."

Gun in hand, the man hesitated a moment as if suddenly adrift.

Emerson glanced at the phone, hoping security was on its way. She tried to stall. "I don't know what friend you're talking about. Tell me the message again."

The man seemed to find his resolve and put the gun to the underside of his chin.

"No! Plea—" Her ears rang with the bang that followed, then all sound was replaced by a high-pitched tinnitus as he fell to the floor.

Emerson dimly registered people running into her office, a few entering for the first time ever. Movement swirled around her. Faces loomed, eyes wide.

"Call 9-1-1!"

She read the shapes of the words on her boss Mr. Fraser's mouth in morbid wonder. With the ringing filling her head, she couldn't hear, but somehow questions bombarded her.

"Who is he?"

"Do you know him?"

"Did he say anything?"

"What did he say?"

Her boss's strong hand took her by the arm and pulled her out of her office. Her balance went funny as she stepped over the legs of the fallen body. The red-and-gray splatter on the wall behind him was surreal, the tangy smell of his blood strangely rich and alluring. She was going to throw up.

She found herself seated back at the break room table in front of the cookies, except now the smell was sweetly repulsive. Mr. Fraser stayed with her. He got her a glass of water she hadn't asked for, and then gave her space by leaning against the counter as he typed furiously on his phone. She wanted her sweater—she was bone cold now—but it was in her office. And she was never going in there again.

A man had just shot himself in front of her. A freeze-frame, millisecond by millisecond, replayed in her mind. The half untucked shirt. A gun in the pocket underneath. His agitation.

A friend sent me.

What friend?

If you want to get out of this alive…

A threat.

The remains belong to the Heolstors.

Which meant the remains probably actually belonged to crazy Thane Ryce Ealdian. Further, she could conclude, definitively, that Bloodkin were not only eccentric and controlling, but they could be extremely violent, too. They were dangerous. She had to get out, and now.

When the police came and asked all the same questions her colleagues had thrown at her, she was ready.

"I have no idea who he is," she said. "I've never seen him before in my life." *Truth.* "He told me if I didn't get off the Kingman Hills mediation project, I would die." A little bit of a lie but a necessary one. She turned her attention to her boss. "By the way, I quit."

The dead man had told her not to repeat what he was telling her about the Heolstors and the remains, and until she felt safe—probably never again—she was staying silent. She'd learned survival early in life. She'd also learned to seize opportunities, and this was one of them.

Ealdian and Heolstor could argue all they wanted. She wasn't about to die for six-hundred-year-old remains like the man in her office.

"I totally understand why you wouldn't feel safe

here," Mr. Fraser said. "Bodyguards have already been hired. They'll be here shortly."

More Bloodkin-hired bodyguards. No, thank you.

One of the cops was persistent. "What is special about this Kingman Hills mediation?"

"You mean besides involving dragon shifters?" she said. "Nothing."

* * *

THANE SHUDDERED IN THE dark, so glad to be home after the recent, unsettling travel. His skin burned with the need to split and shed. His spine arched, shoulders hulking, and he fell to one knee. Braced on the floor, his hand blackened as if he'd been poisoned. His knuckles were forced upward by the claws extending from his fingertips. His hearing sharpened so not only could he hear Matthew's heartbeat as he slept alone in his room above, but also the scratches of insects deep in the earth, and the ocean waves crashing against the Big Sur beach that the Ealdian stronghold overlooked.

And over it all was the Night Song, the strange music that called to dragons. Its melody was one of longing for the dark wind made by the rise and fall of wings. Of all desires, the ecstasy of flight tempted Thane. No gold rubbed between fingertips nor woman taking his weight could compare to the satisfaction the sky promised. Total and utter freedom.

His mind clouded with pain and want. These last months, he'd known the final shift was coming. He'd stopped fighting it. He and Matthew had prepared. The ship to Havyn stood ready in Monterey Harbor. A voyage on the water, and then at last, he would be what he was born to be once more, and go into the night, wind, and fire.

No. Carreen. Rinc. He had something to do for them. For the Ealdian bloodline, the black dragons that went back into the hazy murk of time.

The growl that ripped up his throat wasn't human.

Carreen. Rinc. Heir.

Son.

He filled his mind with the memory of the boy. Just born, Rinc had been so vulnerable and small, lightly covered in a white paste and howling with all his might. The feeling that had burst in Thane's chest—pride, yes, as well as a vast sense of accomplishment, though he knew Carreen deserved the credit—was beyond those simple and selfish emotions. It was soul-changing devotion.

One spellbinding look into his son's enraged eyes and Thane had no longer lived for himself. He was nothing. Rinc was the future, and Thane had wanted nothing more than to give him, on bended knee, the spoils of the Ealdian legacy. He'd also given him his dignity because

Rinc had urinated on him right away. A new emotion, painful in its sudden hugeness, had filled Thane. Where had it come from? Why had it filled him with such terror? Such joy?

The fire within Thane cooled slightly, his throat tightening with anguish. He'd thought that well of tears had dried.

Rinc had left such a vacuum of hopelessness behind.

And Carreen, what a warrior she'd been after all. He would've liked to have seen her dragon. Then maybe he might've understood her better.

The dragon within didn't like regret, so Thane kept his heart and thoughts with his lost family to conquer the beast, discovering that the memory of his son's infant cry could drown out the music of the Night Song. He chose his son over magic again and again, and the hours passed as he fought the shift, the night receding.

Until a faint hiss of movement behind him told him someone was near. Then pain bloomed, something cold and sharp jabbing into his back.

Roaring, Thane stood, taller than he'd been in over a century, his would-be assassin clutching onto him like a tick. Thane's body was still armored with changing magic, so the weapon hadn't been able to go deep, but the intent was clear.

The dragon hurtled into ascendancy again.

Thane reached over his shoulder, grabbed the man by

the neck, and slammed him down on the floor. The weapon—a Drachentöter—clanged to the ground. Designed for slaying dragons, its reverse-facing barbs were still unsprung from the shaft. Few Bloodkin survived the catastrophic damage caused by the thing. Once embedded, it was near impossible to remove, and shifting into dragon form just opened the wounds still further.

His prey still twitching, Thane raked a claw over its belly. He leaned in to rip out the entrails with his teeth.

"My lord Thane?"

Thane spun to face a new attacker, but he found Matthew.

"My lord Thane, remember who you are."

Bewildered, Thane looked back at the assassin, sent by the Heolstors, no doubt. He was still alive but wounded fatally, gore spread wide as he hiccupped, trying to breathe. Thane reached out to him and with an efficient twist broke his neck to end his suffering.

"They sent someone to kill me." Which was no excuse for allowing the dragon to rule.

"You didn't hear him?" Matthew asked with careful reserve.

Matthew would think he'd been listening to the Night Song. "I was remembering Rinc."

He had a duty to Carreen and Rinc, and the Heolstors thought to rob him of it. They'd thought to awaken the dragon and, thereby, leave Carreen and Rinc helpless all over again.

No. This would not do.

Waiting for the DNA results was an absurd Bloodkin Assembly delay. All the Bloodkin knew who'd been found at Kingman Hills. And there wasn't much time left for Thane to do something about it, not with the dragon attempting to wrest control.

"We travel tomorrow," Thane said. "Gerard will answer for this."

"I'll make the arrangements," Matthew told him. "And I'll clean this up."

Thane looked down at the bloody body. The blood *intrigued* him, and the man was already dead anyway. "I'll—"

"No, my lord. Better I do it."

* * *

EMERSON PACED THE BEDROOM of her hotel suite that had been arranged for her not five miles from her own apartment. She resented how nice it was. Its luxury appointments—creamy white leather, chrome, and glass—had been designed to hold light. The bed was low, and the linens had a soft sheen. She bet it was crazy comfortable. It also reeked of money. Dragon money.

They hadn't left her alone for a moment.

No matter how nice the bed was, she didn't think she'd ever sleep again. If she weren't still so shocked over what had happened, she'd be screaming.

The place had been checked and cleared for danger, and a guard would remain on duty all night in the living area. Another would be out in the hallway leading to the suite.

She felt caged, not protected. She'd thought of calling Bryan, but she didn't trust the Bloodkin where her family was concerned. Didn't trust the Bloodkin at all.

Someone knocked on the bedroom door. She frowned at it and sat down on the leather bench situated at the end of the bed, breathing deeply. This sense of powerlessness was unbearable.

Voices murmured in the main room of the suite.

Fine. She'd see what they wanted. Standing, she squared herself and opened the door.

Mr. Fraser immediately stood up from the sitting room's sofa. "Emerson."

She asked the question foremost on her mind. "Did you find out who he was?"

"We did, yes." He gestured to one of the sofas. "If you will?"

Her heartbeat had doubled in anticipation, but she managed to calmly cross the room and sit down. She was having a nightmare. That's what this was.

Mr. Fraser wasted no time. "His name was Jeffrey

Clay. He has no direct connection to any Bloodkin family."

"I don't believe that for a second."

Mr. Fraser pressed his lips together, as if debating, then said, "He *is* survived by a young son who is currently making a miraculous recovery from end-stage cancer."

"What's that supposed to mean?" That the man who'd just blown off his head had orphaned his child? Because she just might lose it. Officially.

"Well, I can't say for sure, but I'd guess...blood." Mr. Fraser's eyes were sharp with meaning.

"Blood," Emerson repeated. So it *was* a Bloodkin?

"Understandable really. What parent, if given the rare opportunity, wouldn't trade his life for his child's?"

And...she was lost again.

"But now the child will have a long, healthy life," Mr. Fraser said.

Because of...?

Oh! Dragon blood.

But that was a myth. A myth!

"You're saying that dragon blood cured the man's child? And the man made a *trade* to come to my office and kill himself in front of me...in exchange for that cure?"

"He delivered a message first. I'm guessing the sender didn't want to be identified."

Her so-called friend.

"None of the Bloodkin wants any involvement with this mediation," Mr. Fraser explained.

She stood. "Who cares what the Bloodkin want? A man is dead."

"But his child lives."

Her boss was being deliberately obtuse. "The world is *full* of people who need cures, but the Bloodkin don't do anything to help them. If dragon blood heals"—*fat chance*—"then dragons are heartless, and I want nothing to do with them."

He looked up at her. "How many people do you think *you* could heal?"

She crossed her arms over her chest. "This isn't about me."

"It is, obviously, very much about you. How many, Emerson? If you were to open a vein and become a walking fountain of health and youth? What would happen to you? Is there anywhere you could hide?"

Fountain of youth? This was getting ridiculous. She wasn't going to get any sane answers today.

"You can't justify what that man did," she said.

"He traded his life for his child's," Mr. Fraser said. "Who wouldn't kill for theirs?"

It didn't matter anyway. "Whoever sent him wants me off the mediation. That was the message."

Mr. Fraser sighed. "Unfortunately, Emerson, that's

impossible."

"A man's head exploded in my office. I'm off it. *You* take the meeting tomorrow with Gerard Heolstor."

"Emerson, I'm not of the blood. Anything having to do directly with the families requires a *Bloodkin* mediator, and the only person we have at this time is you."

"I'm the only…?" Screw that. "Well, the Bloodkin are going to have to be a little more open-minded about non-bloody people, because I'm not going."

Mr. Fraser dropped his gaze to the floor.

"I've been warned away from this mediation several times," Emerson said, beginning to pace, "including by the Heolstor brothers themselves. I'm finally taking their advice. The results of the DNA test should be back in a day or two, and then the whole thing will be settled, anyway." It would take zero effort on his part to wrap things up.

He kept his gaze down. "What about Sadie Couser?"

Emerson stopped dead in her tracks. "Who?" How did he know Sadie's name?

"The young woman you're trying to get into the Desert Valley Treatment Center."

"What about her?" Emerson challenged him. She suddenly wanted to smack him. Had he been looking through her e-mail? Listening to her calls?

"The Bloodkin will see to it that she gets a room at the center for as long as she needs it and that all her expenses are taken care of."

"I already got her in, and I'm covering her expenses."

Mr. Fraser's shoulders heaved with a deep breath.

"You're not serious," Emerson said. Blackmail. He was *blackmailing* her? "No."

"There's only you, Emerson. Gerard Heolstor won't even let me in his house."

"So you actually expect me to go along with this insanity?" She couldn't believe it.

He lifted his head just enough to make eye contact. "You've got the blood for it."

"The man—you know, the one who killed himself in front of me?—he said that *I* would die if I continued this mediation." There had to be other programs for Sadie. Bryan would understand.

"I doubt that very much, Emerson. I don't know what he said to you, but it's unlikely that you'll be harmed. You're a Bloodkin woman. The Bloodkin are very protective of their own, particularly the men of the women."

She sat down in front of him. "The man said *I would die.*"

"Then that threat was a lie. I've spoken to Ransom Heolstor, and he assures me that you will be safe for the duration of your stay at his house."

She rolled her eyes. "Yeah, and when I step outside his front door, I'll be shot in the head."

"Emerson, I swear you'll be safe."

"If you're so sure, how come you have to blackmail me to go?"

"Bloodkin have certain safeties," he said softly, as if embarrassed. "Humans do not."

"Now I'm not human?"

"It's your dragon blood that matters." He lifted his head fully now, and his eyes looked tired and sick. "Human blood doesn't."

Emerson went cold, her mouth dry. She didn't know if there was another threat inside that short statement, but she suddenly didn't think Mr. Fraser had the authority to clarify. She didn't want him to, either. This wasn't up to him.

"You're another messenger," she said.

He closed his eyes. "Yes."

"There's only me." She didn't want her "friend" to spill any more blood on her behalf.

"Yes...*my lady*."

She put a trembling hand over her eyes while she worked on her courage. These were some seriously disturbed people.

Enough. She dropped her hand and addressed Mr. Fraser. "See to Sadie Couser." Her dragon blood made her *his* boss now. She'd probably always been his boss.

"At once." His voice was loose with relief.

Emerson turned back to the bedroom. "And get out.

I need some sleep."

CHAPTER 5

THANE WAS READY TO kick in the front doors of the Heolstor stronghold, but when he brought his car to a stop, Gerard's eldest son, Ransom, was waiting on the great flagstone entry, the massive doors already open behind him. Heolstor strategy had always endeavored to preempt an attack and secure their fortune against unnecessary losses.

But Heolstor would lose much today.

Thane's anger smoldered like acid in his blood as he got out of the vehicle. He made Ransom wait while he took a moment to polish the car door. No scratches for Matthew to have fixed this time.

When he was satisfied, he took the broad steps leading to the house, a flush of anticipation mixing with a deep indrawn breath. The Heolstor stronghold looked out over Napa's gently rolling hills and vineyards, the sun reflecting off the light mist in the air. But despite the serenity of the setting, he was ready to commit murder: first the father, and then the heir—exactly what had been done to the Ealdian line. He'd consider leaving the younger son alive, but if the Heolstor boys were anything like Gerard, then both would fight and both would die. And Carreen and Rinc would know peace.

Ransom had to know what was coming, and yet he seemed unperturbed when Thane reached him. "Emerson Clark is here," he said.

Thane laughed aloud. "You think she'll save you?"

The Heolstor line was hiding behind the woman. Granted, she'd delayed their fate a few days already, but Thane had no problem shoving her out of the way now. Like cowards, they'd sent an assassin to kill him.

"Actually, she's been my hope from the beginning of this mess," he said evenly. "And if we survive it, I intend to marry her."

Thane snorted. "I'll be picking you from my teeth in half an hour. Where's your father?"

He didn't wait for an answer though, just stalked inside to find Gerard himself.

Gerard had always resisted change, and so his

American home had the stone construction of an old world keep. Likewise, colorful tapestries hung from the walls, an adornment that Thane had long scorned. Tapestries could carry fire to a roof in minutes. And what, pray, did dragons breathe? Fools, all of them.

Thane paused in the enormous foyer—sized for a Bloodkin after shifting—and sniffed the air for Gerard, the old beast.

"Where are you?" he roared.

His call echoed up the staircase and bounced down through the gathering rooms on the first floor.

"I'm told he's fighting his dragon," a female voice said. Emerson.

Thane turned to seek her out. Across the hallway and into a spacious, open room he found her sitting neatly in a chair, staring at her mobile device. Matthew had tried many times to press one upon him, but Thane had always refused.

"Sounds an awful lot like a euphemism," she added, not looking up. Her tone was strange, as if both indifferent and angry. Her scent was that bothersome mix of woman and artificial fragrance.

"It means his dragon is emergent," Thane told her. Gerard was older than he by a short span. It made sense that the Night Song filled his mind, as well. Gerard wouldn't be going to Havyn, however. "He will die here, today."

"Tragic, I'm sure."

Her blithe dismissal made him pause. "You don't want to stop me? Ransom is depending upon you to protect him."

The boy had just entered the room, his younger brother behind him. They were both fully grown, but they hadn't crossed their first century yet.

"I'm not here to protect anyone." Her thumb scrolled her mobile's screen, but he couldn't tell what she was looking at.

"Then why are you here?" Thane wanted to take her by the shoulders and *make* her look at him, but the temptation to bury his face at her neck, take a deeper draw of her scent, was too great.

"Gerard Heolstor requested I update him in person."

"And is there an update?"

"No. Nevertheless, here I am."

Something had happened. If he knew women—and he liked to think he did—then this one was ready to draw blood herself, in spite of her seeming apathy to Gerard's imminent demise.

Thane looked first to Ransom and then to Locke. Both of Gerard's sons were frowning, tension in their postures.

"Ms. Clark is here under duress," Ransom said. "Yesterday, someone sent a messenger to her place of work. After delivering the message, he committed suicide in front of her."

Thane shifted his gaze to her. "What was the message?"

Emerson finally looked up, eyes sparking with anger. "*That's* the first thing you ask?"

"It's what is important," Thane said, oddly satisfied that she was snapping back at him.

"A man is *dead*, his child *orphaned*."

"It happens. His message, Ms. Clark?"

Pure loathing radiated from her. "He told me to get off this mediation."

"Upon threat to her life," Ransom added. "Thane. Did you send him?"

"I handle my business personally. I don't need messengers or *assassins* to do it for me," he said. "Besides, she is lying. No one threatened her life."

"Oh, my life was threatened." Her tone seemed to accuse *him* of doing the threatening.

"It makes no sense. Who would threaten you?" Thane shot back. "My quarrel is with Gerard Heolstor. I'll kill him shortly, and likely his sons, but I have no reason to kill you."

"And I may have cause to rip Thane Ealdian's head from his shoulders," Ransom said wryly. "But your head looks lovely where it is."

Her gaze flicked to Ransom and back to Thane. "Comforting, thank you."

Thane laughed. She was the most dangerous creature in the room—no fear, perfect control, and burning from within. Yes, if ever there were a Bloodkin woman to tempt him, Emerson was it.

"Life is brutal, my lady."

"I know how brutal life can be. And I'm not your lady."

He remembered the information Lena had provided about Emerson Clark's background. "I believe you do know something of life's brutalities." *Orphaned and alone. Worst of all, penniless.*

"Oh, save it," she said. "If you're not going to kill me, then by all means, have at each other. I just want to get on with my life." She turned to Ransom. "Is your father ready for me or what?"

"Damn, her fire is up," Locke mumbled.

"Quiet," Ransom told him. He sighed. "Emerson, my father isn't doing well. This close to his shift, some days are worse than others. Will you stay with us until he is a little better?"

"*I'm* not going to wait," Thane said. And he didn't like the idea of Emerson staying with the Heolstors, either. She had too much heat inside for someone like Ransom.

Ransom held up a hand as if to keep Thane in place. "We don't have the results yet from the university. If you fight my father now, the Assembly will condemn you and the Ealdian line."

"No, boy," Thane said. "You broke the law first when you sent an assassin to kill me. I don't have to wait for anything." Godric Tredan of the Triad would absolutely side with him.

"I didn't send an assassin." Ransom looked over at Emerson, and Thane moved to stand in his way. Ransom could not have her. "Or that messenger."

"Gerard did, then," Thane said.

"I swear on the Heolstor line that he did not. He's too far gone. He doesn't care about people anymore."

"Can you also swear that he didn't kill my wife and child?"

Ransom finally went silent.

"Then you won't mind if I ask him myself."

* * *

EMERSON ROSE FROM HER seat as Thane strode past Ransom and Locke into the tall, wide passage that centered the home.

Locke's mouth contracted into a snarl, but Ransom put a hand on his chest to hold him back. "Don't."

Well, Emerson sure as hell was going to follow. She wasn't going to miss her opportunity to inform Gerard Heolstor of where the mediation stood. Then she could get out of here.

Thane paused at the stairs to…sniff the air.

Because that's normal.

She couldn't smell anything, and apparently, neither could he because he continued down the hallway to stand before a set of massive double doors with ornate handles in the shape of arching, winged serpents, a plume of iron fire spitting from their parted lips. Thane grabbed both handles and pulled, but the doors wouldn't budge.

He stepped back, his indigo gaze swinging toward her. "Unlock it."

"Um…?" Emerson turned to look behind her.

Ransom had followed them. "It's no good. The dragon is in control. He'll rip you apart, and nothing will be solved."

Thane shook his head. "I guarantee Gerard is still dominant. Not even these doors could hold a dragon."

Emerson crossed her arms. Her stomach twisted, her decision to follow suddenly swinging the other way.

She didn't like these people, and she didn't want a firsthand look at Gerard Heolstor's state. The smartest way to stay out of Bloodkin business was to stay away from Bloodkin, not go deeper into their houses, looking for trouble. Gerard could come to meet her in that very comfortable sitting room.

"If you won't consider your own safety," Ransom said to Thane, "consider Emerson's."

The man sent a cruel smile her way. "I have a feeling Emerson needs to see Gerard just as much as I do."

"Actually, I'm good." She tried to keep the quaver out of her voice. The Bloodkin had already committed one gruesome crime; she didn't need to see any more, no matter how angry she was over what had happened to the man in her office. "Don't disturb him on my account."

"Unlock the doors, Ransom," Thane said.

She looked at Ransom, surprised to find Locke now standing behind his brother. He was leaning against the wall, his head bowed as if defeated. No, more like he was grieving. Maybe he knew something about Gerard was messed up. Maybe he knew the Bloodkin, in general, were messed up and he was just as stuck as she was.

Emerson turned back toward the big doors just as Ransom laid his hand on a hidden panel, and then a series of metallic *snicks* could be heard from the seal between the two doors.

"Stay behind me," Thane ordered her. "And do everything I say."

She gulped. It was obviously smarter to run away—there was probably a serial killer in there—but a perverse curiosity tugged at her.

He drew open the two huge doors, and a strong smell hit Emerson—bitter and smoky, but with an underlying woodsy scent that she couldn't place. The combination sent a strange, bright, crackling sensation through her body, like the terrified euphoria of a free fall.

Thane shot Ransom a stern look before proceeding

down the large, flat steps. "Gerard, I've come to kill you."

Always to the point, wasn't he?

"What took you so long?" a low croak of a voice answered. "And you brought me a snack."

"That is Emerson Clark, of the Emmerich Reds, and you will not harm her."

Emerson didn't know what a Red was, and she didn't need to. She turned to flee, fresh terror overcoming her curiosity, but Thane reached out and grabbed her wrist. Heat and longing spread from the point of contact. "You're not a coward."

She didn't see why not. Cowards often survived encounters with dangerous people, though she acknowledged that they survived because they let someone else take the brunt of whatever nastiness was in store. And Thane seemed game for nastiness.

He pulled her down with him, and she followed. His vise grip on her arm made sure of it.

The descent wasn't too steep, but the temperature rose markedly with every step. She'd always preferred the cold; heat made her restless and reckless, like late-night summer-break insanity, living fast and flirty. Perspiration dripped down her back and stuck her blouse to her skin. She could feel her face misting, too. And Thane's hold on her arm was positively burning. *She* was burning.

When they finally reached the bottom, a massive

room opened up before them. She couldn't see anyone in the murk, but nevertheless, she somehow knew that Gerard Heolstor was in the dark corner across the space and far off to her right. Something about the darkness…seethed.

Thane swore. "Why didn't you arrange transport for him before this?"

Ransom answered from behind her. "He was all set to take a ship to Havyn, but after he heard about the discovery of the remains, he refused to leave. He said you'd be coming. I think he tried to hold on for you."

Thane shook his head. "No, boy. I'm no motivation for him to fight the Night Song. It's very clear he's been holding on for his sons. To help his sons *survive* me."

Something in his voice—something sad and lonesome—made her think that maybe he'd just changed his mind about killing Gerard.

"Heolstor did not kill Carreen and Rinc," Gerard said in that low, inhuman growl, "just as I know you didn't kill them either, no matter what the rumors say. But if I had wanted to hurt you, I'd have attacked you directly and burned your stronghold to the ground."

Thane dragged Emerson forward. "Did you hear that?"

A near admission in the middle of some more of their trademark crazy? Yeah. She took a deep breath. Time to do her job. "Are you saying that the remains are not from the Heolstor line?"

"Everyone knows who they are," Gerard said.

"Then why the claim?" she asked.

"To buy time. To force Thane to stop and *think* for once. He has always been too quick to fire, the beast on too loose a rein. The fact that Carreen was holding my sigil means nothing."

"*Nothing?* It is the only clue I have. Who did it, then?" Thane demanded.

A figure strode out from the shadows, taller and broader than any man she'd ever seen in person. Under an oddly protruding brow, his eyes were a bright, shining blue, lizard-like in their set and vertical pupils. His bare shoulders were rolled forward, something weird going on with his spine. With a crack like breaking stone, he grew even larger and more hunched, webbing along his upper arms. All power.

Because dragon. Duh.

Gerard pointed a black-clawed finger in her direction. "Ask her."

* * *

THANE GLANCED AT EMERSON, who was vehemently shaking her head, the word *no* formed on her lips but not uttered.

"What do you mean?" he demanded, looking back at

Gerard.

A lick of fire danced in Gerard's eyes. Inside, he had to be experiencing the conflagration of change within his bones, muscles, and blood. He collapsed to all fours, keening with the pain of it. Soon, his mind would blacken with the Night Song.

Thane raised his voice. "What has she to do with it?"

"My sons." The dragon spoke, but it was Gerard who'd chosen the words. A plea.

Gerard was indeed too far gone. Later, Thane would shake the answers from Emerson himself. She had to know something.

Thane didn't take his eyes off Gerard—the fire would overcome him at any moment—so he inclined his chin slightly toward Ransom. "Get Locke. He should be here."

Both sons should be with their father when he died. And after, they would have to consign his body to fire again and again until nothing was left. It was the Bloodkin way.

Thane heard Ransom's footsteps as he dashed back up the stairs, but Emerson seemed frozen in place, her arms clutched around herself.

"Are you all right?" he asked.

She met his gaze, and he found her irises had a green shimmer behind the brown, her dragon peeking out to see one of its own kind. "He's—"

"Going to die, yes," Thane said. But not because of Carreen and Rinc. Because his final shift was upon him, and no Bloodkin, even family, could allow a final shift anywhere near humankind. The final shift was mindless, the man utterly subsumed by the beast.

Ransom and Locke came down the stairs, their treads slow and heavy. The older boy took off his suit jacket and laid it on the stairs, and Locke's breath hitched when he saw his father.

"It shouldn't have been this way," Ransom said, rolling up his sleeves.

No, it should not. Gerard should be a shadow high in the sky, eating atmosphere over Havyn. Instead, he'd had to stay behind to make sure his sons didn't take the blame for a crime they'd been framed for.

"Whoever killed Carreen and Rinc and planted our sigil in her hand robbed him worse than if they'd stolen his hoard," Locke said.

Ransom put a hand on his brother's shoulder. "They'll pay."

"They'll pay in blood," Locke added.

Ransom starting forward. "Let's do this, then."

Thane held up a hand. "You're not strong enough. Either of you." He stripped off his shirt so it wouldn't catch fire. "My dragon is high. I'll do it."

"No, that's *our* father," Locke said.

"I was a father once, too, for a little while," Thane

said. "Give him the peace that he didn't harm you, that his legacy is intact."

Thane could see the desperation in Ransom's eyes, and glancing at Locke, the abject misery in his. They had no other choice. Time, usually a friend to Bloodkin, was no friend today.

Such was the life cycle of a Bloodkin. They were a people with lives as long as the human could remain in control. Yet, with each passing year, the dragon within grew stronger until it overcame the man entirely. Man to beast, beast to fire, and then nothing but ash.

He turned to Emerson. Tears dripped down her face as she clutched herself, scared and solitary. As an orphan, it was unlikely she'd ever witnessed the end change. She was learning all the worst about being Bloodkin first and none of the beauty. And there was great beauty.

Thane approached the semi-formed dragon shuddering on the floor. Gerard was feral in his throes, fire licking all over his skin to char and shed it for the silvery scales that glinted beneath. Already, the knobs of his spine were growing. The hulk of his body quivered, pops and cracks provoking angry growls. His claws scraped the stone floor. Would soon scrape through flesh if he wasn't put down immediately.

When Thane drew near, Gerard snapped at him with vicious, elongated teeth. His wings fluttered, as if fanning fire.

Thane dodged and lunged at the same time, his arms going around Gerard's head. It was too large to grasp with hands on either side, so he had to muscle down and dig his fingers into Gerard's jaw as flame singed his skin. Already, Gerard's hair had been filling in with armored plates, and they cut into Thane's arms, blood slicking his grip.

The dragon thrashed to dislodge him.

"Father!" Ransom called.

The dragon went still for a moment at the sound of his son's voice. And Thane bore down with all his strength and broke Gerard's neck.

CHAPTER 6

EMERSON WAS SITTING BACK in the Heolstor's drawing room, this time with her head in her hands, her elbows on her knees.

Dragon shifters meant…dragon shifters.

And blood and pain and death. But right now dragon shifters were enough to think about.

It meant that one day, that gruesome shift might—would probably?—happen to her. She was going to turn into a really big, fiery monster. Which just seemed insane. There was no way she was one of them. Bloodkin. There had to be a mistake. A test she could take to prove it. She could try to cure someone with her blood. *Oh, God.* She was going to have a nervous breakdown.

"I'm taking her with me." Thane sounded threatening.

He, Ransom, and Locke were still standing in that super-sized foyer. Because people who turned into dragons would, naturally, need super-*dragon*-sized foyers.

Thane had been bleeding badly when he'd nudged her back up the stairs, but most of his wounds had crusted over by the time they'd reached the top. Handy having healing powers like that. A world of non-dragon people *would* want powers like that. Fathers might just trade their lives to get some for their children. Even shoot themselves in the head.

She was going to be sick.

"Someone implicated my father," Locke yelled, "and, because of that, they robbed him of going to Havyn to die proudly as a dragon. I had to watch you break his neck. We've just as much right to revenge as you."

Thane scoffed. "Hardly."

If she weren't so shaken up, she'd suggest that Locke not argue with the man who'd just wrestled a dragon and won. Granted, Thane had gone a little dragon himself— skin weirdly black, eyes shining, shoulder and arm muscles bulging impressively. Locke was no match. The Heolstor brothers together weren't a match for Thane Ealdian.

"Besides, you have to burn your father," Thane said. "Honor him with fire, *then* revenge."

Emerson shivered. The smell of burning flesh was still in her nose, in her clothes, in her hair. She wanted a shower. She might soon beg for one.

"Or would you leave him to rot?" Thane added.

There was a grunting scuffle for a moment, through which she squeezed her eyes shut. *Please, no more death. No more blood. No more dragons, either.*

When silence fell, she looked at them out of the corner of her eye, dreading what she might discover. Thane held Locke in the air with one hand clutched around his neck. Thane hadn't put his shirt back on, so the last of his crusty wounds were visible on his bulging muscles. Her imagination supplied a vision of dragon spines ripping through the skin on his back. Thane might be eccentric, but he had *reason* to be.

"I want Emerson," Ransom said to Thane. "She doesn't need to be caught up in this Blood feud. Taken advantage of. I'll marry her today, if need be."

She pressed her lips together in refusal. Not that he wasn't a catch or anything—handsome, rich, scaly on the inside—but she was good solo, thanks. Besides, his brother's face was turning an uncanny purple. Ransom should probably do something about that.

"Emerson was finished with you the moment Gerard admitted that the remains discovered at Kingman Hills are those of my family," Thane said.

Actually, Emerson thought, she was done with the

entire mediation when Gerard had admitted that, so there was no reason for her to hang around. She just had to find that damned driver the Bloodkin had hired to bring her from the airport and get the hell out of Dodge. Now was as good a time as any.

She stood, legs a little wobbly, bag on her arm, and walked across the room with as much composure as she could manage. Her weight on the balls of her feet muted the sound of her heels on the marble floor in the foyer. She was already grasping the front door's handle—another snaky dragon—when Thane stopped her.

"Where are you going?" His voice had that low roll deep within it. She knew now that the burr belonged to the dragon part of him.

She gulped but didn't turn around. "I need some fresh air. The smoke was—"

"You stay where you are," Thane said.

"I'm not letting you take her," Ransom said from behind her.

"*Letting* me?" Thane growled. "Gerard said she had my answers, and I'm having them whether you like it or not."

Taking advantage of the distraction, Emerson opened the door and slipped outside. They could argue all they wanted, but she was her own boss now and she'd do what she liked. Right now, she wanted to run away. Unfortunately, the Bloodkin's car and driver were nowhere to be seen.

She speed-walked around the house toward the separate bank of garages she'd spotted when she'd arrived. Her car was probably there. Keys, too. And her driver, if she were lucky.

Under no circumstances was she ever going back in that house. Come to think of it, she couldn't go home, either. The Bloodkin owned her building.

She fumbled in her bag for her phone. She'd call Bryan. He'd help her. And he'd probably laugh at her for not believing in dragons in the first place. She sure deserved a good ribbing…after a stiff drink, a good cry, and a lot of therapy. Because dragons…. She'd seen one break another's neck. The mere memory of the sound of cracking bone made her cringe.

The garage was labeled CARRIAGE HOUSE—Bloodkin sure liked fancy names and titles—and there seemed to be a small office inside. She knocked on the door, and then tried the handle. Happy day, there was her driver with his feet up on a table watching television, a soda in hand.

"If we can be on the road in thirty seconds," she said, "I'll give you five hundred dollars." Company money.

Her driver stood and grabbed his coat from the back of his chair.

"That won't be necessary," Thane said behind her. "I'll drive."

The driver looked crestfallen. Emerson felt the same way. How had Thane crept up so quietly?

"That's very kind of you, Mr. Ealdian," she said, jerking a nod at her driver to get him moving, "but I have a ride."

Her driver took a step toward the garage door.

"It's Thane," he told her, then turned to the driver. "Five thousand dollars for you to sit back down again."

Emerson scowled at the driver as he wavered a second, stepped back, and then traitorously lowered his butt back onto his seat.

She held out her hand to the driver. "Give me the keys."

"Emerson, you have to come with me," Thane said in that scary low tone of his.

No, she didn't.

The driver put the keys in her hand. She might forgive him, after all.

Taking the side door into the garage—six cars were neatly situated side by side—she pressed the fob to locate hers.

"Can I help you?" came a voice from the back. Some Carriage House servant maybe?

"I just need my car, thanks," she called.

"Emerson." Thane took her arm. "Someone killed my wife and son."

Like a slap, the truth of the statement hit her. *His wife*

and son. If dragons were real, maybe he *was* directly related to remains that were six hundred years old.

She froze in place, suddenly uncertain.

"Yes," he said harshly. "They were—*are*—mine. I must discover who hurt them, who *burned* my little boy. And if you can help me…"

Those remains had been his family. Someone had murdered them. Like her, Thane had been left alone in the world. He was in pain. She didn't understand the Bloodkin, but that much she knew. *Oh, God.* She was such a pushover.

She turned to him, and for the first time, really looked at him. Thane Ealdian's eyes were as full of feeling as a stormy sky. The indigo color flickered with firelight from within, the vertical pupils like upheld daggers. His expression was drawn tight over features that were rough in their beauty—that full, tensed mouth, high cheekbones defined by such strain, brows angled with tension. His was the face of a desperate, angry…well, dragon.

As close as he was, towering over her, broad shoulders blocking the door, she was acutely aware of him as a man. Had she actually laughed at him once?

She couldn't help shaking. "Look, I don't know how you think I can help you. I have *no idea* what's going on."

"And no idea where you came from, either."

"Ignorance is bliss." She was sure of it now.

He gave her a circumspect once-over, and his gaze

felt like a scorching sun on exposed skin. "No, not for you. You're Bloodkin through and through."

"Look, I don't even think I *am* Bloodkin. I think there was a mistake. I don't feel like a dragon." She mostly suppressed a hysterical laugh. "And I don't want to. That shift was horrible."

"It didn't have to be," Thane said. "The shift is usually...*rapturous*. Fast and hot. Freedom you can't imagine until you've taken to the sky. You've got the Blood. I've seen the dragon in your eyes." He paused. "No, don't shake your head. I have."

"I would know if I were a dragon." She'd said the same thing to Bryan.

Thane pulled her even closer, and heat the likes of which she'd never known—velvet, caressing, sensual—moved over her skin. "And what will you do when the dragon grows stronger? When the Night Song touches you."

So close. Too close. "Night Song?"

He leaned down, mouth to her ear. "My lady, the night will call to you. How will you fight it? When it's time, how will you get to the safety of Havyn without the aid of the Bloodkin?"

She dropped her gaze to the concrete floor, still shaking her head. She didn't believe it, couldn't. Night Song? Havyn?

And damn, it was so hot in here. She tried to put a

little space between them.

Thane allowed her an inch. *"Hic sunt dracones,"* he said. "Here be dragons. It's on a few very old maps but is nevertheless difficult to find."

Maybe Bryan could help her find the answers. Or would the Bloodkin come after him? Make him shoot himself in his head to protect their secrets?

She dared to look Thane in his extraordinary eyes. So what if it sent electric shocks along her nerves? "I was very graphically warned that I would die if I continued with the mediation." Specifically, if she didn't say the remains belonged to the Heolstors, which apparently, they didn't. "A man killed himself in front of me."

"You're not a coward," Thane said, his upper lip curling with satisfaction. Why did he keep saying that? "Nor easily bullied."

Bullied. She hadn't thought of it that way, but, yes, someone had tried to bully her, and in the worst way possible. How stupid of her not to realize it.

"I'm terrified," she admitted

"Not the same thing as being a coward."

"I saw a dragon today." She wasn't over it. Not nearly.

Thane smiled. "And wasn't he magnificent? You should see one sky bound."

Her heart lost its beat. "Are you going to kill me?"

His smile faded and he gave a reluctant shrug. "I hope

not. I'm near my final shift, too. I can only promise I'll keep my distance when the Night Song tempts me."

It wasn't much of an assurance, but she really did like how honest he was. Lots of crazy, but no bullshit.

"I still don't know how I can help you," she said.

"Think," he told her. "You're the keystone in the bridge between me and the one who murdered my family."

That sounded ominous.

He leaned in again. "Who seems to know more about you than you know about yourself?"

Emerson thought back. There was no one in her life who knew... *Wait.* "Mr. Fraser." He'd even admitted to being another messenger. And he'd called her, *my lady.* Which had been weird coming from him.

Thane pulled back a smile, fierce and feral, his lightning eyes flashing. "That's where we'll start."

* * *

THANE TURNED ON TO an open road and pressed his foot to the gas.

"I'm just going to say it since I'm probably going to die anyway." Emerson was gripping her seat.

He heard her heartbeat accelerate as she held her breath. His heart beat faster, too. While in seclusion, so many things had been blotted from his mind by the

Night Song—memories, purpose, sensations as a man perceives them. Now, stimuli beat him constantly, and he relished every impact. For example, Emerson's too-sweet fragrance had grown slightly earthier with her sweat and stress. He took big lungsful of Emerson-scented air to clear his mind.

"Yes?" Thane tilted his head toward her, waiting for her to continue.

"You have no business behind the wheel of a car."

"I've missed flying." It'd been a century at least since he'd dared become a dragon to enjoy the ecstasy of flight.

"Well, fly in the sky, buddy. Puny human beings have only so many years to live, not your six hundred."

Where had she gotten six hundred? *Ah.* "I was rather middle-aged by Bloodkin standards when I took Carreen as my wife."

She gaped at him. "How long do you people live?"

"You people? *We* live as long as we can control our dragon. The human is dominant early in life, and so we usually shift for the first time upon reaching maturity. Over time, however, the dragon becomes more ascendant, and it's not safe to shift, especially near human habitations."

"And this will happen with me?"

"Yes, when you're ready." What a strange woman she was, alternately fearless and vulnerable. She seemed to be able to brave just about anything, except when it came to her identity, and then she was lost.

"You mentioned Emmerich Reds earlier," she said.

When he was introducing her to Gerard, yes. "A long time ago, the Emerson name was Emmerich. Your dragon will be deep red, like the summer sun when it is low on the horizon."

At her silence, he glanced over to find her looking out her window. The Emmerichs had been a proud line. Pride had killed them...almost. Where had this one come from?

"What do you know about your background?" he asked.

"Apparently, nothing."

"You knew enough to apply to the Bloodkin for tuition money for your studies."

Her gaze whipped back to him so quickly he almost laughed. There was her temper.

"You checked up on me?"

"Of course. I have good reason. What do you know of your heritage?" he asked again. The clue to his riddle could be in the mysterious appearance of an Emmerich after so long.

She gave an exasperated sigh. He was discovering that her nature had a flare for drama.

"When I was little, a visiting step-uncle mentioned that I was a dragon shifter. It's supposedly why I was such a pain in the ass. Anyway, it stuck in my head. One of the only things I can remember from that time, actually. When I was applying for financial aid, I checked the box. That's all it was—a checked box—and I got a free ride, plus a generous stipend for living costs. I still think—and have always thought—that someone made a mistake."

She clung to her doubt. It would not save her. Doubt never had that power.

"The Bloodkin don't make mistakes like that." He turned on to an open highway, the better for speed. "Someone would've immediately investigated your background and confirmed that you have dragon blood in your veins, and he or she made the decision not to inform the rest of the kin. Of course, your name helped to obscure your identity. Clark isn't a Bloodkin surname, and Emerson isn't a female first name."

"All I got was a letter on Bloodkin Assembly letterhead specifying the amount of aid. No other information."

Now he had some questions for Godric. "Why would you be given information? Knowledge is power, and we dragons like power just as much as we like wealth. Someone is using you, and we are going to find out who."

"I still don't get why I'd have anything to do with your wife and child."

He was going to scare her again with what he had to

say, but he had to say it. "I think you were offered to me as a replacement for Carreen. Young Bloodkin women are rare and in high demand."

Her eyes widened in horror.

"Oh, don't worry," he said. "I'm declining, or didn't you notice?" It didn't matter that he enjoyed her company or that he *wanted* to touch her. "You're lovely, intelligent, and have an intriguing spark in your eyes, but I won't be placated with a hasty and convenient substitute for Carreen. Whoever killed my wife and son will pay in equal measure."

"I was *offered* to you? So women are just things? What's the word you ancient folks use…chattel?"

Ancient folks. She made him sound so old, when he felt younger than he had in ages. "It's not like that, not among the Bloodkin. Sending you was strategic. To keep the peace." How could he make her understand? "It's like arranged marriages. Their purpose is strength and prosperity. My union with Carreen was arranged."

While they had not understood each other, they had created Rinc. What a magnificent future they had held in their hands—that squalling, angry little tyrant.

The dragon stirred within, made restless by a flare of fury.

Thane realized Emerson was watching him, smoothed his expression, and released his death grip on the steering wheel. Rinc. He had to change the subject. "What do you know of your parents?"

Emerson stared at the road in front of her, a hand now braced on the roof of the car.

"Not much. Both my parents are dead. I was adopted by a good friend of theirs—Jillian Stevens—and then when *she* died, I got passed around her family. No one really wanted me. I don't blame them. I wasn't even related. So when I got to be too much trouble, social services took over." She hesitated for a moment. "I'm sorry about your wife and son. You must have loved them very much."

Again, the dragon moved under his skin. Thane's foot pressed harder on the accelerator.

He tried yet another topic. "*Your* taste in lovers could use some work. A dog? Really?"

"Is that why you had Matthew follow me? To see who I was meeting?" She didn't seem embarrassed though. These modern women.

"I had Matthew follow you because Bloodkin have never been safe on their own. The general public may not believe in dragons, but many others do." He paused, considering, but decided to tell her everything. "I asked Carreen's sister Lena to look into you. She was the only other person who searched for Carreen and Rinc with me, who believed Carreen hadn't purposely run away."

Emerson was silent, and the dragon was so restless within him that he stopped fighting and tried talking about it. It almost seemed as if his dragon *wanted* her to know.

"Carreen denied the dragon within her. Some choose to never shift and at the end of their lives, suicide as a human before the dragon overwhelms them. And I...I reveled in the strength and boundlessness that I found in my dragon form. No one crossed me. No one stole from me. Few looked me in the eyes. She was afraid and had reason to be, though she did her duty. She was an ill-matched wife, perhaps. But a mother to the bone."

The silence between them grew, and that old despair tightened around him again, making it difficult to breathe. He'd given Carreen everything, but he couldn't give up his dragon. It was inside of him. It *was* him.

Heat rippled over his skin, like the promise of ecstasy without the release. All this time, and he was as lost as he'd been before. No pleasures could satisfy him. No amount of gold would make him smile. The value of everything had been rendered to dust.

"Bryan is not a dog, by the way," Emerson said after a while.

Thane smiled slightly. He wasn't sure, but he thought she was trying to make him feel better.

"He's a wolf shifter, and he's my brother. Foster brother. He was going to help me get away from you crazy Bloodkin, though I don't see how that's really possible anymore. Not if I'm going to change into a dragon someday. I wouldn't want to eat any…villagers or anything."

Now he knew she was trying to make him feel better. The corner of his mouth lifted into a smile. He hadn't expected kindness. She didn't owe him that.

"So you were going to run away from yourself, were you?"

She dropped the hand that was braced on the roof. "Please don't start making sense. I don't think I can handle a Bloodkin making sense."

Her wry way of coping eased the rest of his discomfort. She was easy to be around. Her nearness settled his dragon. He'd make sure she was safe and established by the time this business was over and he left for Havyn.

"I thought we were going to see Mr. Fraser," she said. "SFO is that way. You missed the exit."

He shook his head. "I'm taking you home. If Fraser serves the Bloodkin, he will come to us."

CHAPTER 7

"W E MEET AGAIN, MR. Chandler," Emerson said as she climbed out of the car, grateful for the solid ground beneath her feet. Thane had cut a three-hour drive to Big Sur down to a little less than two. His place overlooked sheer rocky cliffs that went straight down into the ocean below. The salty air whipped through her hair. The silver sky beckoned, and for a moment she envied the gulls winging out above the water.

Chandler gaped at her and then looked to Thane, stricken. "My lord?"

She grumbled at his response, but the edifice Thane called his "stronghold" captured her attention.

Apparently, that was dragonspeak for *big-ass castle*. Majestic in its size, classical in architecture, and spare in embellishment, Thane's home was an estate both large and grand enough to house the government operations of a small country. The massive double doors were flanked by sculptures of Roman warriors. She doubted they were reproductions.

"Emerson will be assisting me in my search for Carreen and Rinc's killer." Thane gave the hood of the car an affectionate pat as she imagined a rider would his horse. "See that she's comfortably situated, and buy whatever clothes and things she requires for her stay."

Mr. Chandler shook his head. "I'll find her a place in town."

"No. She needs to be here. When does Fraser arrive?" Thane joined her in front of the steps leading up to the house.

Mr. Chandler was speechless, but his eyes twitched as if he wanted to keep arguing.

"I'm sorry for the inconvenience," Emerson told him. "It'll only be for a few days,"

Thane's brow lowered.

"Maybe a week?" she amended. Definitely not longer than that. "I'll stay away from...um, *his lordship* at night. I'll binge on television. I'm behind on all my shows."

Mr. Chandler was ashen. "You have no idea the danger you're putting yourself in."

Thane growled at him. Actually *growled*.

"Oh, but I do," she said. "I just witnessed Gerard Heolstor's end change." She marveled at how she sounded as if she knew what she was talking about. "Thane broke his neck right in front of me."

"And who will kill my lord Thane if the Song overcomes him?" Mr. Chandler asked.

"You will, Matthew," Thane replied, low and dangerous.

"By pricking you with my short sword?" Mr. Chandler impatiently gestured to a sheath under his suit jacket that she hadn't noticed before. "I think not."

He had a *sword*? Emerson shook her head. By now she shouldn't be surprised by anything these people did.

"I'll be long gone by the time that happens, I promise," she said. She hoped it wasn't wishful thinking.

She glanced at Thane for confirmation and found his gaze heavy upon her. He almost appeared normal in the half-light of early evening. The weight of his many centuries on Earth was lifted by pale shadows so that he now *seemed* as young as his face and body looked. She realized he wasn't really young or old. Somehow those words didn't seem to apply. He was just Thane. Timeless. Ageless. Magic. The world turned around *him*.

The impact of the concept made her stop in her tracks. Being unaffected by time was a kind of freedom she hadn't known existed, couldn't even really fathom with her measly twenty-five years, and yet it seemed this freedom was hers now, too. How long would *she* live? What kind of life could she have?

"When is Fraser coming?" Thane asked Mr. Chandler again, though he didn't shift his gaze away from her.

Her mouth went dry, her face hot.

"Tomorrow at ten, my lord."

Under Thane's intense scrutiny, she pivoted slowly. "Mr. Chandler—"

"Matthew, please," the man corrected.

"Matthew. I'd love a shower, please, if it's not too much trouble." She was still so smoky, and she needed to think. And she couldn't do that if Thane wouldn't stop looking at her.

Matthew motioned her toward the stairs of the enormous porch. "This is a bad idea."

She followed him into the house, but she was aware of Thane, *dragon shifter*, at her side. And now she had a better idea of what that meant, just not exactly what it meant for her.

The main room to Thane's stronghold was enormous and built of white stone befitting a temple. Arranged on an oriental area rug, the furniture—a dark leather sofa, chairs, and a large table—were solid in their design. Another sculpture—this one a female, primitive in its smoothness and gestural composition—stood to the side of the sitting area. Naked and full-figured, she stood regally, her only adornment the curls on her head and a low crown over her brow. She exuded strength, boldness, and blatant sexuality.

Thane came up behind Emerson, his body heat warming her skin.

"There are some cave drawings of possible dragon shifters," he said, "but *The Goddess* is the first known depiction in art. She was discovered in Mesopotamia in the Royal Cemetery at Ur."

Emerson looked closer. What she'd thought had been a crown was actually a series of protrusions of bone on the woman's forehead—nascent spines?—not unlike those Dr. Buckley had pointed out to her on the skull of the female remains from Kingman Hills. *Carreen, Thane's wife.*

"I could be like this?" Emerson asked, more to herself than either Thane or Matthew. There was no way this ancient woman was or had ever been chattel. She was more like an aloof queen, full of power and tranquility at the same time.

"Emerson," Thane said, "you are already like her. And you will be utterly terrifying when you know it for yourself. I pity the Bloodkin man who attempts to win you."

Thane thought she was like this queen? Not nearly. She was trying, though. It'd help if she weren't so scared all the time. But give her a thousand years, and maybe she'd get close.

"I don't want to marry a Bloodkin," she said to cover her embarrassment.

"They will want you," Thane said. "Ransom Heolstor does already."

Her mood cooled. *Ransom. Mr. I'll-marry-her-today.* "Then he's going to be disappointed."

Thane smiled. "You prove my point."

Something passed between Thane and Matthew, and the latter said, "This way, my lady."

He led her up a marble staircase, though she still felt Thane watching her from below. Even when she turned the corner into the hallway, she felt him. The house— simple and strong—was an extension of him.

Matthew settled her into her room and had dinner sent up. Shortly after, a few packages arrived, filled with some basic attire in the sizes she'd specified to Matthew earlier. The pajamas were the comfortable and soft variety, her favorite. She curled up in bed with her tablet and watched television, one episode rolling into another while her attention slipped sideways. Night fell, and she should've been sleepy, but the air seemed to vibrate with a strange intensity that made her restless. And yet, the anxiety that had pursued her for the last year working for the Bloodkin was gone, unable to penetrate Thane's domain.

The strange sensation made her want to go outside to

take a walk in the moonlight, but the memory of Gerard's shift kept her in the guest room. Thane had warned her. Opening the window was the best she could do to satisfy the longing that pulled at her heart. But even the salt-touched wind seemed to have substance. Outside, the summer scent was thick with growing, blooming things. The waves of the ocean roared and hissed in her mind. The stars here shined brighter, as if she could reach up and gather them by the handful. She felt more alive than she'd ever been before.

Was Thane making her feel like this? Or was *her* dragon finally waking up?

Morning found her sitting on the floor, her back to the door. She'd closed her eyes but hadn't slept, concentrating instead on how the sunlight from the window crept up her body in a blanket of gold.

When she finally rose to dress, she didn't have to look in the mirror to know that her eyes would be different. She knew already. As she expected, a citrine green had overtaken her usual brown. And she now had twin daggers for pupils, too.

* * *

THANE STARED AT MATTHEW in disbelief. His long-time man-at-arms had just taken position next to *Emerson* after delivering Martin Fraser from the front door to the chair set aside for him for their meeting. Matthew had been at *Thane's* side since long before they'd taken a boat to the New World.

"I'm not dead yet," Thane said to Matthew. "You could at least do me the honor of waiting to find a new master until I'm gone. I shan't be too long, I promise."

Though, come to think of it, Matthew could do far worse than Emerson, and she'd need someone knowledgeable to advise her as she came into her own among the Bloodkin.

Matthew's mouth tugged upward. "I anticipate fire, my lord. I'm just making certain the lady doesn't get burned."

Thane raised a brow, then shifted his focus to Fraser.

The man's heartbeat was rapid, and he stank of fear. Thane was making him wait. *The better to break him.*

Fraser's gaze flicked from face to face and settled on Emerson's. Her blazing eyes didn't seem to put him at ease, but Thane felt tremendous satisfaction at her dragon's emergence. The blue blouse she wore made her skin glow, and she wore pants that fit her perfectly. Hers was an effortless beauty, and her figure was damn distracting. His dragon was focused entirely upon her, and so, he had to admit, was the man.

"How was the flight?" she asked Fraser.

"Fine, thank you," he answered. "Though, I'm a little confused as to why I'm here. As I explained to you, I cannot advise on the matter of the Kingman Hills claim." He gave a nervous laugh. "I don't have the blood for it."

He was being deliberately obtuse. Thane would smoke him out soon enough.

"Oh, the claim has been settled," Emerson said. "The meeting with the Heolstors was very productive. The remains belong to Mr. Ealdian, although both he and the Heolstor brothers kept talking about revenge and blood and war, so the repercussions of the discovery seem inevitable."

Her eyebrows lifted to imply impending mayhem, which made him want to smile. She'd had that effect on him from the beginning.

"Then why am I here?" Fraser asked.

"Mr. Ealdian thought you might be able to answer a few ancillary questions to tidy up all the details."

Fraser's gaze slid over to Thane, and he withered slightly.

"Of course, I'll help in any way I can."

"Good. Let's begin, then, shall we? To whom do you report?" Thane asked, forcing his attention on Fraser.

"I report to the Assembly." Fraser bowed his head. The posture reminded Thane of when vassals used to kneel to him. Some of the Bloodkin families still required that kind of subservience.

"Specifically, to whom do you report on the matter of Kingman Hills?"

"You, my lord, and Gerard Heolstor, or either of his sons if Lord Heolstor was unavailable."

Something about his voice was familiar. *Ah...yes.* Thane remembered Fraser now. A couple centuries ago, there'd been a tobacco venture and he had handled the details of the contracts between the parties involved. He'd seemed competent enough back then. Dragon blood must have sustained him over the years, just as it had Matthew.

The question was, whose blood?

"Anyone else?" Thane asked.

"No one," he said. "Your kind depends upon discretion."

A lie. Thane gave him a tight smile. "You're not leaving without giving me the answers I require." Thane doubted he was leaving at all, and judging from the sweat that dripped down Fraser's neck into his shirt collar, he knew it, too.

"I am nothing without loyalty. I've proven myself time and time again," Fraser said.

"Proven yourself to whom?"

"All of you," he said.

Thane glanced up at Emerson.

"Mr. Fraser," she said.

He looked up at her, then remembering his place, down again quickly.

"Am I an Emmerich Red?"

Fraser exhaled in an easy whoosh. "Oh. *This* I can speak to, if only in a limited capacity. The Triad believes you are, yes. A sample of your blood was tested to confirm dragon heritage. Until you shift, however, we won't know for certain what line you're from. At such time as your Emmerich heritage is confirmed, the Emmerich hoard, properties, and accounts will be transferred to your keeping."

Thane lifted a brow at Emerson while addressing Fraser. "The hoard was maintained all this time? By whom?" Fraser started to answer, but Thane, remembering an old alliance, beat him to it. "The Herrera line. Has to be."

Emerson shook her head slightly, mouthing. *Hoard?*

"Every dragon has a hoard, Emerson," Thane explained. "It's in our nature to…acquire. I'm sure you have one already."

She gave him an exaggerated frown and shook her head.

Oh, yes she did. Hoards in popular mythos were often imagined as riches, but in reality they were filled with *precious things*. The monetary value was secondary.

"The Herreras were Emmerich allies," Thane said. He should've thought of them before. "If the Herreras maintained the hoard rather than subsumed it within their own, then they had to have had reason." And if they'd known that an Emmerich still lived, why the secrecy? Emerson's life could've been so different.

She looked astounded. "I have allies?"

Fraser shook his head. "We don't know where you come from yet. You have *to shift* to know for sure. Your dragon will answer the question definitively. The Herreras, and indeed the rest of the Bloodkin Assembly, have been very patient."

"Oh…well," Emerson said, "I'm deeply grateful for their forbearance." She sounded anything but.

Herrera. Were they the ones Thane was looking for? Had they killed Carreen and Rinc?

No. It didn't feel right. He'd had no quarrel with them. In fact, they'd always lived on different continents and pursued different business interests. They'd prospered on intellect and wise alliances, not violence. What cause had they to attack Ealdian? Why would they send an assassin six hundred years later?

Perhaps Lena would think of something that connected them.

"Why didn't you tell me this before?" Emerson demanded of Fraser.

Thane had told her why already: power. The Triad had been trying to keep her in check.

"It wasn't mine to tell," Fraser said.

"You're awfully chatty about it today," she shot back.

"You asked me directly. And I assumed that Mr. Ealdian had informed you about your family."

Her voice rose. "My family? You know *nothing* about my family." She lifted shining, confused eyes to Thane. "All this time. Even when I was in college and already identified as Bloodkin. It's been *years*."

At her distress, his dragon flexed within him. She'd been alone. She'd made a wolf her brother. She'd had to ask for money to learn, to live. Her anger was his anger, too. He knew what it was like to be alone.

"I don't want the hoard, whatever it is, whatever it's worth," she said. "And I'm *done* with Bloodkin. What kind of *ally* would leave me to fend for myself at *seven*?"

"It's possible they didn't know your circumstances," Thane said. He'd find out if they had.

Emerson shook her head. "It doesn't matter. I don't care. I'm done. *Sooo done*. You people make me sick."

You people. No matter how much she wanted to, she couldn't will her dragon away. Her eyes were brighter and greener than ever.

She walked toward *The Goddess* and stood looking into her serene face.

"Emerson, you're not alone in this," Thane said to her back. When she drew away—or drew into herself—his dragon became agitated. He needed her here with him. "You're not alone anymore." The Herreras would be made to acknowledge her identity. Did they know what had become of her parents?

She turned abruptly. "Can we just finish this? I need

to take a walk."

Yes, maybe that was the better course. Finish, then talk.

Thane was turning back to Fraser when a flash of steel preceded a high, ragged cry.

Fraser gripped his arm as blood squirted from his wrist. The white bone and red flesh of his forearm was exposed by a clean cut. His severed hand lay on the carpet clutching a gun.

Matthew held his short sword slightly away from his body, blood dripping from the blade.

"Not again." Emerson's face and lips had gone white. "Oh, please God, not again."

"He wasn't going to shoot himself, my lady," Matthew said. "He was aiming for my lord Thane."

* * *

"PLEASE, I NEED DRAGON blood." Fraser's face was white with strain.

Nausea curled in Emerson's belly. She knew now why the Bloodkin called themselves that. Somehow, they kept managing to spill blood. The smell—rich and metallic—made her throat tight. Thane, on the other hand, moved closer to Fraser.

"I'm not going to give it to you," Thane said to him. "Not after you just professed loyalty to my kind and then tried to sting me with that weapon. To what end? A bullet wouldn't kill me. To provoke the dragon?"

"I had to try," Fraser said. "If I didn't, I was dead anyway."

Emerson frowned in disgust. "Who put you up to it?"

"I'll tell you if you help me," Fraser said. "My hand can be reattached. It will grow back together. I've seen it done. *Please.*"

She hated all of them. "I want to know who put me on the mediation."

"You'll heal me if I tell you?" He looked so pale, but she couldn't bring herself to care.

"Yes." Of course, she would've tried anyway because she wasn't a monster like the rest of them. Revenge and blood and war. That's what Thane wanted, and by now, she knew to take him at his word.

"Lena Orvyn," Fraser said.

Thane took a step back as if struck. "No. You lie."

Lena. The name was familiar, but Emerson couldn't place it.

Fraser nodded and looked at Thane. "She told me to assign Emerson to the mediation and to keep her involved at all costs."

Emerson glanced at Thane, too, whose teeth were...*sharpening* as he shook with rage. The skin above his indigo eyes was deepening to gray. It seemed like they knew the culprit after all. Lena Orvyn. Now maybe this could end. Nobody else had to die.

She approached Fraser to save his damned hand. Disgusting. "Matthew, I don't know how to do this." Open a vein? "Can you help me?"

Fraser reached out toward her. "If you just cut—"

And then his head fell off, hit the floor with a soft thud beside his hand, and rolled to expose a rictus of surprise.

She blinked twice, but still didn't understand what she was seeing. She looked at Matthew, who was lowering his sword again, fresh blood sliding down the blade. The corpse of Martin Fraser leaned slowly forward but was held morbidly upright in the chair by its deep seat and high arm.

"My lady," Matthew said, "he betrayed two dragons today, my lord Thane and Lena Orvyn. I wasn't letting him near a third."

* * *

"NO, I TOLD YOU I'm done," Emerson said when a gentle hand touched her shoulder. Matthew's. She'd collapsed on a chair at the big table, her head buried in her arms. She was getting out of here as soon as she could stop shivering.

They were so violent. Why were they so violent? All this death. Some things were starting to make sense, though. How *had* Thane managed to live so long if not by killing everyone in his path?

She stole a glance at him from across the room. He was weirdly crouched low and rocking on his feet, a strange, savage purr coming from his chest. Thane was battling inner demons, she could tell. The impulse to go talk to him, talk him back to himself, collided with the instinct to survive, to stay away. She didn't know what to do.

"You need to go back up to your room," Matthew told her. "Now."

The sharp, red blade, still clutched in his hand, continued to drip on the floor. The carpet was ruined already, so she might as well vomit on it, too.

Thane bellowed in pain, strain making the tendons on his arms, shoulders, and neck stand out. His shoulders were rolled forward like Gerard's had been before he'd caught fire, before he'd shifted. She'd known Thane was close, but now he seemed on the very brink.

"Go now. Please." Matthew took her under the arm and yanked her to standing.

And then, suddenly, he was knocked out of her sight, and Thane loomed large, a smoky musk wrapping around her as he dragged her down to the floor with him. She screamed as he caged her between his arms and legs. His very pointy teeth were not an inch away from her neck, his breath so hot it singed. And there he stayed, trembling above her, but not attacking.

Her body flashed hot in response, something within—her own personal fortifications—crumbling at his nearness. She was vulnerable and in the clutches of a man-monster, but she had no idea which part was dominant.

"Matthew?" she called, her voice a little high and thready.

The barrier between her and Thane was breaking. She didn't know what would happen if it collapsed entirely. He was so close, so raw. And in her own way, she was, too. This was dangerous.

"He grabbed you." Thane's voice was barely human, but he wasn't taking a bite…yet. "I can't trust anyone. I thought I could. But if *she* betrayed me, then…"

He had to be talking about Lena Orvyn, the woman Fraser had named. She must be really bad news for Thane to lose it like this.

Tentatively, Emerson tried to look past him and spotted a black boot and its very still leg on the other side of the room. "I think Matthew is hurt."

"He'll live," Thane said. "I can't move. Not yet. Not safe."

"*He* was trying to get me to safety."

"You're safe here. Safest here. With me." His body was shaking.

She was alone with a man at war with his dragon, so

she was pretty sure her safety was questionable at best. But as the seconds ticked into minutes, her heartbeat slowed and her breath evened. Underneath the smoky darkness of the dragon, he smelled like a morning shower, clean and fresh but tinged with a note all Thane—a combination that wasn't bad, not really. His warmth relaxed her tensed muscles. Melted her.

She discovered that she wasn't afraid. Not really. Who better to protect her from an emergent dragon than Thane? Yeah, even if the dragon was him.

She trusted him. For the first time in forever, she trusted someone.

"I don't like all this death," she finally said.

His forehead touched hers, another tremor rolling over him. "I thought Lena was a friend."

"Is she your...?" *Lady friend? What do dragons call sweethearts?*

"No. She's Carreen's sister. She searched for Carreen with me, remember?"

She nodded. Yes, she remembered now. He'd mentioned Lena during the drive on the way out here.

"Did she know about Rinc? Did she take Rinc from me?" The turmoil in his voice was too much for her to take.

"I hope not," she said. "But we'll find out." Emerson had some questions for her, too.

"We'll find out." Thane seemed to hang on to that

promise.

They'd hang on together.

Silence fell, and still Thane kept her close. When his tremors finally abated, Emerson spoke again. There was a dead body ten feet away, and the iron tang of the blood was making her sick. "Could you maybe keep me safe elsewhere?"

He inhaled hugely, as if breathing her in. "Yes. I know a place."

He ungracefully slung her over his shoulder and carried her through the house, down some stairs, and palmed a security panel, which opened a door. They descended into darkness, and she deeply regretted asking to move…until lights flickered on one by one across a cavernous room. She had an upside-down view of a cache of riches the likes of which she'd only seen in movies.

Holy cow.

"This is your hoard," she said as he set her down.

The neat piles of gold bars were almost cliché, but seeing them in person made it a truly extraordinary experience. He had art displayed on the walls—masterpieces, no doubt—and texts in covered cases. How he'd managed to get a car down here—a fancy old Mercedes—was beyond her.

"A safe place," he said, sounding more like a sad, exhausted version of himself.

A bank of high-tech safes lined one wall. She nodded slowly, in awe. "For serious treasure."

He smiled and met her gaze. "And precious things."

CHAPTER 8

"SHE MUST BE REALLY bad news," Emerson said.

Thane slid his gaze to the floor. "I've been blind."

Lena. She was why he'd never discovered Carreen and Rinc. *Lena* had hidden the truth, and he'd never once suspected her. He'd been a fool to believe her grief and desperation.

Carreen would find a way to send me a message, Lena had assured him. *She'd have to be trapped for her to be silent so long.*

But who *would hold her?* Thane had demanded a thousand times. *Why?*

He'd thought it had to have been an enemy to the Ealdian line, or else they'd have spared the babe. He'd

121

never considered a sister who hated the other so much that she murdered her child, too.

He was ashamed to remember wondering if everything would've been different if he'd married Lena and not Carreen. He'd merely agreed to the contract. Marriage was business, and Carreen had done her part. Lena married later and had her own son. He'd had no reason to suspect bitterness between the two.

"Will you stay here while I check on Matthew?" His man-at-arms had been silent too long. "I promise I'll come back."

Emerson seemed to be trying hard to keep herself together, and Thane appreciated it.

"Can I look at all your cool stuff?" Her voice had a tremulous quality she couldn't entirely hide. He didn't blame her for wanting to run away anymore. Carreen had hated violence, too.

"You might like what's in there." He pointed to the vault on the far right and told her the code. He'd never told anyone a code before. Never. Not even Matthew had unrestricted access to the hoard, and he'd never been left alone in the vault.

"I won't steal anything."

"You'd better not." He tried to sound lighthearted, but it came out rougher than he'd intended. Oddly, he'd give her anything she asked for. He didn't know why, except perhaps because the stars would soon be his treasure, and the sky would be where he kept his hoard.

Yet here he was, turning to go back through the security door, leaving more or less a stranger behind. When he closed the door after him, locking her in, the dragon within settled contentedly, uninterested in the scent of blood and the sudden availability of fresh meat. The dragon was satisfied, while Thane was in pieces.

He found Matthew sitting against a leg of the table, pain creating lines of stress across his forehead and around his mouth. But since he was awake and had moved, the healing process had to have begun, years of Thane's dragon blood mending what he had broken. But it seemed Matthew's back was still injured since he wasn't standing or moving his legs.

"Does Emerson live?" Matthew sounded devastated.

"She's fine. I put her in the vault while I came to check on you."

Matthew narrowed his eyes. "You've never lied to me before."

And he wasn't now. "Emerson Clark is currently admiring my collection of royal jewels. I gave her the code to the safe before I left. She says I have cool stuff."

Cool stuff. He liked that.

"You gave her…?" Matthew blinked at him stupidly. "Have I died? I've died."

Thane shook his head. "You'll probably outlive me. Actually, once I go to Havyn, I really do think you should serve Emerson. She'll need you."

"I'd planned to die with you, my lord."

The old way. The beloved servant going into flame and ash with his master. In modern times, it was rarely done, but then again, neither he nor Matthew was a modern man.

Thane couldn't turn down this gesture, not after everything he and Matthew had endured together. "I'm honored, friend. It's decided. We'll find another way to help Emerson take to wing."

"She's so—"

"Beautiful, I know. And brazen. And smart." What a dragon should be.

Matthew lifted a brow. "I was going to say heedless. My lord, you are smitten."

Smitten, yes. What a bittersweet ache it was with all the other turmoil in his heart. It'd been a long time since he'd wanted anything. "You're smitten, too."

Matthew closed his eyes and shivered with pain. "She was so irritated at me when we first met, I couldn't help it. And you seem more and more like your old self."

Felt like it, too. The dragon within was smug.

"Ransom Heolstor wants her," Thane said.

Matthew affected a small shrug, another improvement. "Strong line. And Ransom is intelligent."

"If I had more time…" Thane didn't finish the sentence. The thought behind it was uncomfortable.

Matthew would understand anyway.

"Correct me if I'm wrong, my lord, as I've only served a dragon these past several centuries, but I was under the impression that Bloodkin have all the time they want."

Thane was shocked for a moment at the idea. He could have her, if he was strong enough. In fact, the dragon wasn't putting up much of a fight. The dragon had…changed its mind?

"If I take Emerson for my own," Thane said as Matthew carefully stood and then toed the severed hand of Martin Fraser, "we may not be going to Havyn. There will be no fire or flight for either of us any time soon."

He'd fought the Night Song for so many years and had almost lost to it, but he couldn't deny that his dragon was now interested in another mistress—an end to loneliness.

How strange that Emerson should arrive in his life when Carreen and Rinc had been discovered, their murderer named. A little sooner, and Thane would've refused to see her. A little later, and he'd be fire on the wind.

Matthew stooped, grunting, to pick up his short sword. He wiped the blood from his blade with a handkerchief. "She might be disinclined to accept your suit, my lord."

"You don't think she'll want me?" He was Ealdian, a black dragon, royal among their kind.

"I didn't say that. But you do lack finesse."

That stopped him. "Finesse."

"And patience, my lord."

"All dragons are patient," Thane argued. It was how they watched their riches grow. Compound interest.

"She's not just another woman to warm your bed, my lord. She's a Bloodkin, the heir to her line. I won't lie to please your vanity."

"Heaven forefend you should," Thane mocked him. "Pray, how do I win the dragon maiden? Since you are such an expert?"

Matthew sheathed his blade, ignoring Thane's sarcasm. "For starters, don't announce your intentions. Considering her introduction to this life, she'll refuse you outright."

"I wasn't going to." Yes, he was. He'd thought to tell her straight-out in case she *had* been considering that boy, Ransom Heolstor.

"You might compose a sonnet. Commission her portrait, perhaps. Find an undiscovered flower and name it for her."

"I don't understand how those things will get her naked in my arms." Which, truth be told, was an immediate goal.

Matthew made a disapproving sound with his teeth and tongue. "You are too motivated by fire, my lord."

"I'm a dragon, and so is she." It didn't help that the

scent of Fraser's spilled blood was fuzzing the edges of his mind.

"She's also a woman of rank. *Woo her.*" Matthew lifted a hand. "I'll say no more. I'll wait before I cancel the arrangements for Havyn. We may be going there yet."

"You have so little faith in me?"

"You've gone a bit wild these last few weeks, my lord. You're not in any form for seduction. Carreen and Rinc's remains were just discovered, you have a debt to settle with Lena Orvyn, and now you want to pursue Emerson? These passions are all born of fire."

"My dragon won't harm her." He'd taken her to his hoard, after all.

"Fire is fire," Matthew said. "It burns."

"You dare a lot to speak to me this way."

"I'm not afraid of you, my lord Thane. I'm afraid *for* you. Tread carefully. You have everything you want within your grasp."

And both the past and future on balance. Yes, he understood. And Matthew was the only person he'd hear it from. Fine. "I suppose you won't let me eat Martin Fraser?"

Matthew merely looked at him.

"*Hmph,*" Thane grumbled. "But you're the one who killed this one."

Thane returned to the vault. He descended slowly into the temperature-controlled, fire-safe lair where he stored his hoard. *Patience*, Matthew had said. *Woo her.*

Thane's dragon disagreed. Vehemently.

Emerson was sitting on a pile of his gold, a Habsburg crown on her head, rubies and emeralds strung from her neck, large bracelets like unchained manacles on her wrists, and a strand of pearls doubled up and wrapped around an ankle. Her eyes were puffy and red from crying, their color back to their human brown.

She's also a woman. Damn Matthew to hell for being right. Revenge and seduction were not good bedfellows.

"I take it you found something you like?" Yes, he wanted her. To see the world through her eyes. Kiss her. Lick her skin and taste the salt of her sweat.

His dragon stretched in anticipation, but Thane forced it down. *Not now.*

"I figured, why not?" she said. "Bryan said I was royalty. And royalty wears crowns 'n' shit."

Hmm. This wolf brother of hers might be an asset, after all. "He was right. Among shifters, you are." Red and black dragons together would be wonderfully terrifying.

Thane knew that she was distracting herself from what had happened upstairs with Fraser, but she'd come around. *Patience.* He had so little.

"Why do you even *have* jewelry?" she asked. "*You* don't wear any."

"It seems I acquired it for you."

She gave an inelegant, tear-clogged snort. "Oh, please. They're useless." She shook her head. "No, don't look at me like that. They are. Just sitting here in your vault. And no one can really wear them anywhere, either."

She would. And nothing else. In his bed.

He approached slowly and sat on a nearby stack of gold bricks. Any closer and he'd be too tempted. "Why don't you tell me about *your* hoard."

"I don't want it," she said.

"Not that one," he amended. "Yours. Every dragon has a hoard. It's in our nature. A collection, maybe? My first, when I was a child, was smooth rocks from a stream on the Ealdian lands. I still have them around here somewhere." Locked in a vault. *Mine.*

"Rocks."

He nodded. "Smooth ones."

Something shifted in her gaze. Half her mouth tugged up. She'd thought of something.

"Are you going to tell me?" he asked.

Emerson shrugged. "Since I received my Bloodkin windfall in college, my cupboards have always been full to bursting with food. I never have an empty refrigerator. And it's all mine."

Thane concealed a shudder of dragon rage. She'd been hungry at some point in her life. Very, very hungry. The Herreras had much to answer for.

"And what's your favorite?" He couldn't help but ease

closer where her scent was thicker.

"Chocolate," she said. "And cheesecake. And cookies, or…I used to like cookies."

"A sweet tooth." He could work with that.

"Yeah. Every bite is an epic battle between my willpower and my waistline."

And the spoils of that battle would go to him.

"Matthew makes an excellent cheesecake." He didn't, but he would learn. Immediately.

Her gaze finally met his and held. "So he's okay?"

"Yes. He's fine. Up and walking about, doing Matthew things." Like cleaning up another dead body.

"He healed because of your dragon blood?"

"Yes. It's kept him with me for a very long time."

"And he's served you? Basically forever?"

Aside from the bodies, it wasn't *that* bad. "He's amassed a small fortune himself. He could choose to go off and—what do you say these days?—live large. I wouldn't hold him, nor begrudge him anything he wants."

"But he stays."

"Sometimes time moves so fast that you hold on to what is steady. To what you know. And from there, safely look out at the world." Only years passing, one upon another, could teach her that.

"Look out at all the death, you mean."

Thane paused for a moment. "Martin Fraser's life had

been extended, as well."

She frowned deeply. "He didn't deserve to die like that, no matter how long his life had been extended."

"He did, Emerson. And Matthew was quick and efficient about it. Fraser came into my stronghold intending to shoot me in the back."

Her lips puckered, considering.

Thane wanted so badly to kiss them. "And he told me about Lena, which will end her life, too. Fraser didn't have that right. He never had that right. His extended life gave him innumerable privileges; all that was required was loyalty."

He swallowed, coming to terms with the discovery of Lena's treachery. It was *his* fault for not seeing it before. Where was the one place he hadn't searched?

"Well, does it get any worse than this?" Emerson sounded like she couldn't take much more.

Nevertheless, he gave her the truth. "My revenge will be complete. I will have Lena and her heir, regardless of his innocence."

Emerson hissed and shook her head. "I meant does *dragon life* get much worse, but I guess you just answered that, too. Yes."

"I will mete out justice. And it *is* justice. She burned my infant son, or she concealed the one who did." He touched Emerson's chin to hold her gaze. "But yes, it gets worse. If dragons are rediscovered by humanity, you will learn how bad it can be. We were once hunted to the brink of our extinction, and only secrecy and quiet living protects us. That is the mission of the Assembly."

"I don't know how you all manage *quiet living* when you like blood so much."

You all. She still didn't think of herself as a dragon. She needed time, he reminded himself, and he would try to give it her, but it was a fight against his dragon he didn't think he could win for long.

"Blood is tempting, yes. And fire, too," he said. "And freedom and flight. But we like prosperity more. And it's there that the Bloodkin makes their peace."

She looked wary and tired, but he pressed her anyway. "Will you let me show you?"

She watched him for a long time, a little flash of green showing in her eyes as she considered. Of course, she had no idea that he intended to take all of her, not just her trust. But he was a dragon, so she shouldn't be surprised when she found herself thoroughly possessed by him. A dragon took what it wanted. Took and *kept.*

Finally, she nodded. "Yeah, okay. I hate not knowing anything."

He tried not to smile too broadly as he reached for her hand. She squeezed his tightly, and with that small movement, she sealed her fate.

* * *

"I'M SO SORRY I didn't return your call," Emerson said to Bryan, the phone lodged between her ear and shoulder as she carried her suitcase down the stairs. "Things got sketchy. Real sketchy." And were going to get worse, if that were possible.

Lena Orvyn had some explaining to do.

Matthew sprinted up the steps to take the suitcase from her, grumbling, "You couldn't wait one minute?"

"Who's that?" Bryan asked. "What's happened?"

"Bloodkin insanity is what's happened," Emerson said. "But I'm okay." *Barely.* "A dragon shifter is helping me out. That was his, um, right-hand man." She wasn't going to call Matthew a servant. And since Matthew shot her a smile as he took the suitcase out the front doors to the car, she guessed she'd labeled him correctly.

"What dragon shifter is helping you out?"

Bryan was family, so she decided to go ahead and tell him. "His name is Thane Ealdian. He was involved in that mediation I was working on in Santa Barbara."

"Thane Ealdian." Bryan sounded surprised.

Uh oh. "You've heard of him?" She stepped outside into the morning sun and squinted.

"Yeah, he's something of a legend," Bryan said. "Old dude. Badass fighter back in the day. Is he the one who killed his wife and kid?"

"They were murdered, but not by him," Emerson

said. *Geez.* "But he *is* old." She tried not to stare at the way Thane filled out a pair of jeans. He was leaning up against his shiny black deathmobile, waiting for her. His arms and chest were doing merciless things to his shirt. "Positively decrepit."

Thane smiled, and she flushed. Big day ahead.

"Ember, I have a bad feeling about this," Bryan said. "You wanted out."

"Your bad feeling is warranted. Two people have died recently regarding the mediation." Her stomach was leaden even as her heart fluttered erratically at random moments. This time she was deliberately going in search of Bloodkin mayhem rather than it finding her. She wasn't sure the turnabout was an improvement.

"Three," Thane said as he walked around to the driver's side. "The assassin."

Oh yeah. "Three," she told Bryan while mouthing a thank-you to Matthew, who'd just slammed the trunk shut. The trunk was apparently in the front of the car, not the back.

The plan was to hear what Lena had to say. At the very least, she'd betrayed Thane by withholding information about his wife and child. At worst, she was directly responsible for their deaths. Emerson would get answers to her own questions, as well. And then Thane would decide what to do from there. But Emerson knew vengeance against Lena and her heir—a two-hundred year old man who lived in Vegas—was probable. The son first, so that Lena would know Thane's pain. And then he'd come back for her. Very medieval. No, older than that. Old Testament.

Emerson prayed this Lena woman was not the one who'd done this to him.

"Dammit, Ember," Bryan said. "I want you out of there. Now. You can come to me, or I'll find you. You need to get away from them. I should've listened to you in the beginning. I'm sorry."

Just the fact that he was offering to help meant so much. "No need to apologize. I kind of sprung the whole Bloodkin thing on you. If I need help, I'll call you, I promise. How's Sadie?"

Matthew opened the car door for her and she got inside. Thane revved the engine and she shook her head at him. *No speeding.*

"She's settled," Bryan said. "Getting the five-star treatment because of you."

"Least I could do." At least some things were falling into place. "I want to visit her as soon as this business is finished."

"I'll go with you. We can get the pack together again."

"Sounds perfect." It was everything she'd hoped for. Her family. "I've got to go."

"I'm texting you my address, just in case."

"I'll keep you posted."

"Ember, be careful."

"You, too," she said and ended the call. Then she frowned. She'd been so focused on her situation that she'd forgotten to ask him about his Alpha and how they were getting along. *Next call, definitely.*

Thane flipped a tight U-turn and headed down his long driveway, spitting dust and gravel behind them.

Emerson scowled as she grabbed for her seat belt.

A toothy smile spread across his face. "*Ember* is it?"

"You could hear that?" Was there any privacy among the Bloodkin?

"The dragon hears all."

Hers didn't. At least not yet. "Good to know. Mental note: no calls in front of Thane."

"I got what I wanted, anyway."

"And that is?"

"A name that suits you. *Ember.* It's perfect. The spark of the dragon is there, within you. All you have to do is blow."

CHAPTER 9

THANE'S AUTOMOBILE SKIMMED OVER the miles, but this time he didn't try for a memory of low, smooth dragon flight. He kept the speed under ninety and was rewarded by Ember—yes, that was her name to him now—relaxing back into her seat.

She'd done something to straighten her hair this morning, which he still didn't understand, and she'd selected a blouse in a deep, Emmerich red, which he did. She had her pick of jewelry—the finest the world had to offer—but she wore only small gold clips on her earlobes and a thin gold chain hanging from her neck.

Yesterday they'd talked for a long time, sitting there

surrounded by his hoard, and eventually Matthew had descended carrying large floor pillows. Trays of food had come later. Wine, too. Thane hadn't even minded when Ember had invited Matthew to join them.

"Aren't you lonely?" she'd asked Matthew. "Don't you want your own life?"

"I have everything I could want: a long life *and* a family. My great-great-grandson just graduated from Harvard Law last week." Matthew had grinned proudly. "I follow the lives of fifty-three of my descendants and have helped out here and there when they have gotten into trouble. I love social media because I get more access than I've ever had before."

"Social media," Thane had said. Those words made no sense together.

Emerson had ignored him. "Do they know who you are?"

"Not really," Matthew had answered shrugging. "A wealthy relative. I'm vague on the connection."

"Do you plan on getting any of them involved with the Bloodkin?" she'd asked. "Is that allowed?"

Matthew had inclined his head to think about the question. "Allowed, yes, but not everyone is suited to the life."

"I don't think I'm suited to it."

"Say that again in a hundred years, my lady," Matthew had answered. "I think you'll have changed your mind."

Thane had disagreed. "It won't take a hundred years. You'll change your mind after you've flown in the sky for the first time."

How he envied her. His dragon might be content with Emerson's company, but Thane wouldn't be able to chance shifting again, flying again, until he went to Havyn. And now he had no idea when that might be. He'd have to satisfy himself by watching Ember take to the night sky and indulge in the joy *she* found. Not long ago, he'd have found such a thing intolerable, but now…he looked forward to it. He could give up flight if he could have her laughter for his own.

He merged onto the highway heading to the mountains, and it twisted before him like a graphite scribble on the world.

Beside him, Ember heaved a huge sigh. "I'm so freaking tired and wired at the same time."

"Wired," he repeated. He really had to catch up on the jargon of her generation.

"Zapping with energy, old man," she said. "Not necessarily a good thing. I'm having trouble sleeping lately."

Too much death, he thought. She needed to get all this behind her, and then she would rest more easily.

"What does the Night Song sound like?" she asked.

Or maybe not death. Something else.

"Sound is only part of it," he said. It was dangerous to

contemplate the Song with the yearning still just beneath his skin, but he wouldn't hoard information from her. "The Night Song is the cacophony of all living things, the silence of darkness, the glow of the sun reflected on the moon, and the chorus of the stars. It is the caress of air and the shimmer of heat, an altogether bonfire of sensation."

"So much feeling," she said, "that it's impossibly hot, right? I feel like I'm going to explode."

"Your dragon is stretching inside you. Looking out. Wanting more."

She gave a shaky laugh. "I don't think sleeping pills help with that."

No. Sex did, but since he was still being patient— *damn Matthew*—he wouldn't suggest it. Yet. Soon, though.

"After we complete our business with Lena," he said, "you might consider attempting a shift."

A line formed between her brows. "So…is the first shift usually done alone, or does another Bloodkin show a beginner how it's done?"

He chose his words carefully so as not to hurt her feelings. "It's usually a family event."

Event didn't do justice to the private celebration that was more extravagant and exclusive than a wedding. Only the closest and most important kin were in attendance. Expensive gifts were brought, the young drak—male or female—feted in style. And upon the third night of feasting, everyone gathered and shifted together.

She'd gone quiet, so he tried to fill in the gaps where her kin should be. "You'd want your Wolfkin foster brother present, I imagine?"

She blinked. Her eyebrows went up, and she smiled. "Oh. Yes. I guess so. I've seen him shift a few times, so I guess it's fair."

Thane didn't like that she'd witnessed such an intimate thing, but the wolf had stood by her, so he set it aside.

"And Matthew would be honored," he said. "He's quite taken with you."

She grinned. "I like him, too. Okay."

Thane caught her looking at him out of the corner of her eye.

"I hope you'll be there," she said.

"Of course. I'm hosting the party," he said. The Herreras would not be invited. They'd kept her Emmerich heritage from her for too long. And the Heolstor brothers might wish to come, but he couldn't tolerate one of them flying with her. *Mine.*

He knew just what to gift her, too. Something without price. Something dear.

"You'd do that for me?" Her eyes were full of feeling. "I don't know what to say. Thank you."

"You should have so much more." He couldn't help that his voice came out in a low rasp. Truth sometimes forced its way into words. His dragon wanted to curl around her and keep her close, striking at anyone who dared come near.

After a moment, she leaned over toward him, and pressed her cool lips to his cheek.

A shudder of desire rolled through him—not sexual, not here or now, on the brink of a confrontation with Lena, but certainly one of anticipation.

She wiggled a little in her seat and rested her head against the window. Only when she was breathing deeply did he look at her. *Ember.* The name fit so well. She was the last ember of her bloodline, a white-hot jewel hidden in the ashes of time.

She slept as he drove, her eyes moving behind her lids, her dragon at peace.

* * *

JUST AS HE HAD a few days ago, he stopped his car in front of Lena's stronghold in the mountains. The place was silent, as if deserted. The sequoias were still. No birds called to one another. Even the dust kicked up by the wheels of his automobile seemed loath to swirl and settle.

"Looks like no one's home." Ember opened her car door, but he put a hand on her arm to stop her from getting out until he was by her side. He appreciated her modern independence, but today he was going back to the old ways.

"Oh, she's home," he said. And waiting. All these years, Lena had to have known that sooner or later he would come for her. What could've possibly transpired between the sisters that she'd not only taken Carreen's life, but Rinc's, as well?

Thane strode around the car to Ember's door with calm determination. He gave her his hand to help her to her feet…and keep her behind him.

"This doesn't feel right," she said, following him up the front steps.

"No, it does not." The place felt too aware.

When they reached the front doors, he didn't bang on them—if they were going to be opened for him, her staff would have done so already. The latch gave easily in his grip, and he pushed one of the doors open.

The sharp metallic scent of blood wafted outside in a billow of escaping air.

"Oh God," Ember said behind him. She must've scented it, too.

Spilled blood. Again. What did the violence here mean? Had Ransom Heolstor beat him to vengeance?

"Thane?" Ember gently pulled back on his arm as if to keep him from entering. "This feels like a trap."

"We do not retreat," he said. "We are dragons."

"I thought dragons were supposed to be *smart*."

"It's smart to kill our enemies when the chance presents itself. And besides, the answers we seek are inside."

Thane entered cautiously, the scent of blood thickening until his lungs felt coated in it. A pall of death shrouded the house. He'd known that his family's remains would mean war among the Bloodkin, and it seemed that the Orvyn stronghold had been the first to fall. Lena's allies would most certainly strike back at whoever had attacked here today.

"Lena?" he called.

The silence was broken by a distant intake of breath, followed by a cracked whisper. "Godric." The voice could only be referring to Godric Tredan of the Triad. *What had he to do with anything?*

Thane pulled Ember close. Two steps into the manse, and the air whistled so high only a dragon could hear it. Thane was already turning, pushing Ember out of the way as a Drachentöter darted toward him. It missed his chest, but the weapon pierced his shoulder above his heart. The barbs sprang from its shaft, burying the steel inside him. The starry burst of pain blacked his mind for a moment, but the dragon within could see everything clearly.

Another assassin. The dragon hadn't heard a heartbeat, so this one had to be dead already.

Thane trained his pain-blinded gaze high to his right.

Braced preternaturally in the corner of the ceiling, his assailant's normally gray skin was rosy from feeding, his eyes gone demon bright. His heart did not, could not, move in his chest.

Vampire.

* * *

"FIND LENA," THANE COMMANDED in a growl.

Emerson hesitated. His indigo eyes were lustrous with intensity, the ridges of his forehead becoming more pronounced as his skin tone deepened. But there was a spear piercing his shoulder—it had to hurt—and some kind of spidery-looking man on the ceiling. Another assassin?

The freak launched himself toward Thane, who ripped the spear from his body and swung it just in time to connect its shaft to the creature's belly. The assassin flew back on impact, slamming into a grand piano, his nails scraping across the black lid and then coming to a sudden stop. With a leap, he crouched weirdly on the wall, as if gravity had no hold on him, ready to pounce again.

A dangerous purr rolled up Thane's throat as his shoulders rolled forward. He glanced over his shoulder, and Emerson staggered back. "Find her for Rinc," he said.

Right. They'd come to get answers from Lena. And if Thane was…occupied, getting them was left to Emerson.

She backed down the entry, no idea where to look, then listened to a darkness moving inside her, urging her toward blood. Strange and frightening sensations beat at her skin, erotic heat and primal glee, as she sought the heart of the violence. Some part of her was feral, too. She couldn't deny it now.

The body of a man—a servant, Emerson guessed—was sprawled in the hallway, a sharp weapon still in his grasp while he swam in a pool of red.

"It wa…" the voice whispered again from deep within the house. "Godric."

Emerson didn't know who Godric was, but she had a feeling she and Thane would be visiting him next. Anyone whose name began with *God* was bound to have issues.

She edged around the puddle of blood and headed in the direction of the voice. Thane roared from the front of the house, and a huge crash shook the walls, dust misting down from a crystal teardrop light fixture into the air.

Yet another body—a young woman in a service uniform—blocked a short hallway into what Emerson guessed was the kitchen, so she went around the other way, through an enormous sunny dining room with a long table surrounded by at least twenty chairs. There she found a huge sunroom at the back of the house, with an open door leading to the outer lawns.

Pinned to a wall with one of those spiky spears through her chest was a beautiful woman with auburn hair, jewel-gold eyes, and a crown of knobby bone under the skin on her forehead. Her arms were slack, the inside of her lips coated red. She'd apparently tried to run but hadn't gotten far.

Emerson rushed to her. "Lena Orvyn?"

Another roar and crash from the front of the house made the windows shiver in their panes.

Dragons were supposed to be able to heal on their own, so…should she pull the spear out? The weapon seemed to be deeply embedded in the nicely papered wall. It would take dragon strength to pull it free.

"Can you shift?" Emerson asked.

"I can…die," Lena gasped, as if she hoped death would come soon. The effort it took to form the words, the very breath needed to give them voice, told Emerson that Lena was not going to survive this, no matter how well dragons could heal.

Emerson had so many questions, but Thane's were more important. "Did you kill Carreen and Rinc?"

"No. Nev—" The last word was overcome by a thick, liquid wheeze.

"Was it Godric?" Was that what Lena had been trying to tell them since they'd set foot in the house?

"Yesss." A drip of blood coursed from the side of

Lena's mouth down her chin. "Wanted Carreen. Always."

This Godric had wanted Carreen, who was Thane's wife. *Okay. Simple enough.*

"I...helped"—a shudder passed over Lena—"Carreen. Meet him."

Thane had said that his was an arranged marriage. That Carreen had done her duty. But maybe she'd also gone after the man she'd truly wanted...

"Carreen wanted Godric, too?"

Emerson took Lena's next shudder for a yes.

"But Godric was jealous, anyway?"

Lena managed a trembling nod.

This was so messed up. Thane had said that arranged marriages were about peace and prosperity, but it seemed to her like they sucked all-around. Big-time.

"I'll tell Thane," Emerson said. Maybe he could forgive Lena for keeping the information from him, since she was now dying because of it. "Thane will make sure Godric pays for what he did to your sister."

Lena closed her eyes and tried to shake her head. Blood ran more freely from her mouth. "It's..." She choked on a word and then tried again. "No...good."

"What's no good?"

Lena's eyelids trembled, but only the gold showed. "Godric..."

Emerson held her breath.

Lena's next syllables were unintelligible glubs, but her

final dying words, enunciated with intense exertion, made Emerson sick with dread. "Godric…sss…*father.*"

Oh hell.

Suddenly, it made perfect sense why Lena had hidden this information from Thane for hundreds of years and then tried to interest him in another Bloodkin woman—keeping Emerson on the mediation—when the remains were found. Emerson was tempted to hide this information from him, too. Carreen had been unfaithful with this Godric bastard, which was bad enough, but that Rinc wasn't Thane's son? That was just brutal.

CHAPTER 10

THANE'S LEFT ARM HUNG limply at his side, blood from his shoulder washing hot and steamy down his body, soaking his clothes and pooling in his shoe. The Drachentöter had done most of its work, maybe all. His mind and vision were hazy, and a terrifying weakness was easing up his spine. The dragon thrashed within to take over the fight—and as a dragon, Thane could win it—but at the same time, he would lose everything. Lose himself in his final shift.

No, this was a man's fight.

He hated vampires, the parasites. But they made excellent, if expensive, assassins since it was difficult to kill what was already dead. Thane grasped him by the neck as the vampire lashed out with his sharp claws. Deep, angry cuts opened along Thane's good arm and shoulder, even his face, but his clammy flesh didn't—couldn't—feel much.

With the last of his strength, he pinned the vampire to the floor, knee to the assassin's chest, sternum cracking under his weight. Squeezing hard, Thane crushed his throat, but that wasn't good enough. His grasp slid to just under the jaw, and he forced the chin up until he felt the bones in his neck come apart. Muscle, tendons, and skin ripped as the vampire's head finally came off.

Dead now. Forever.

Thane wavered momentarily above the corpse, but as blood flowed from his wounded shoulder, the room dimmed, pinpricks of light—not stars—gleaming momentarily before fading as he collapsed forward on top of the headless body.

* * *

"THANE!" EMERSON SQUATTED DOWN, grasped him around his ribs, and heaved, rolling him off the body of that freak—who was now dissolving into noxious goo, but she was not going to think about that—and onto his back.

Oh-God-oh-God-oh-God.

Blood covered his left side, sourced by the wet burble at his shoulder where that spear had struck and ripped into him. She put her hands to the oozing wound and pressed to stop the bleeding, but the red just seeped through her fingers. Dragons were supposed to be able to heal, but all Thane's wounds—and there were many— were open and livid, his skin tone gone pasty where it was visible.

Her nerves were frazzled with alarm, but her mind narrowed with intense focus. This was *not* the time to fall apart.

He was cut and bleeding from just about everywhere, but his shoulder—too close to his heart for much hope—was the main problem.

She surveyed the room and fixed her attention on the curtains. *Pull them down, rip them up, dress the wound.* In one swift movement she left his body and got to work. The fabric was a thick, silvery-blue brocade, but for some reason she had no problem tearing it into fat, long strips.

"You're going to live, Thane Ealdian," she said as she used all her 130 pounds to pull him up to a sitting position so she could wrap the cloth tightly around his chest as a bandage. Blood soaked the material, but when she was finished, the outer layers were dry.

Laying him back down again, she put her ear to his face to see if he was breathing.

Come on...

Then she searched for a pulse in his neck and was rewarded by the faintest of taps against her fingertips.

Please, hang on.

"If you die, you can't throw me a party. And no one has ever thrown me a party before, so you kinda have to live," she said, hoping to get a reaction out of him. She didn't give a damn about the party.

Next. Matthew. He'll know what to do.

She grabbed for her bag and located her phone. She found his name and hit SEND—the brilliant man had thankfully had the presence of mind to program his number into her mobile—then she put it on speaker while she felt again for Thane's pulse. Still there.

The mobile rang and rang, but no one picked up.

Come on…

She ended the call and tried again. No answer.

Cold dread rattled her. Lena Ovryn's staff appeared to be dead, and an assassin had been waiting for Thane and her to arrive. Maybe Godric had sent someone to Thane's house, too. Maybe Matthew was lying in a pool of his own blood, now lost to his fifty-three descendants.

Her vision blurred with tears, but she shook them away. She couldn't think about Matthew now. Thane needed help.

Bryan. She selected his name, hit SEND and SPEAKER again, and when he picked up, she was talking before he had a chance to say hello.

"Thane's hurt badly, maybe fatally." No, he would live. She'd make him live.

"What happened?"

"A Bloodkin is after us, some grand master bastard named Godric. He's been killing everyone involved with that project I was working on."

"Are you hurt?"

"No."

"In immediate danger?"

"Probably. But Thane killed the last guy here."

"Where are you?"

Emerson had to make herself think. Her thoughts were caterwauling out of control. "The mountains. Not quite Lake Tahoe, but in that general direction."

"You have to get out of there."

No kidding. "I have Thane's car. I'll—" her mind raced "—find a motel nearby. Take care of him there. Can you come?" If Bryan could get on the road right away, it'd take him a few hours to get to her. "I don't know what to do for him, and he's not healing on his own."

A hospital was *not* an option. They'd just take more of his blood. And hers. Then all the Bloodkin's.

"If he's wounded that badly," Bryan said, "the best you can do is get him somewhere *safe*. He'll either heal or he won't. I think you should bring him here."

No. "That's *hours* in the car."

"But you'll be in my territory. I know my territory. If

some Bloodkin is after you, I can take care of you better if you're here than if you're in a random motel room somewhere. Thane will be safer, too, and if he dies, I have to be able to protect you."

Bryan had no idea how badly injured Thane was. She was staring at the gruesome wounds, her nerves screaming on his behalf. "He won't be able to make it that far."

"That's Thane Ealdian you have there. If anyone can make it, he can."

"Bryan, you don't understand. He's out cold. Some freaking spiky spear thing ripped up his shoulder."

"A Drachentöter?"

"A what?"

Bryan sighed. "A dragon slayer, a weapon designed to kill Bloodkin. Damn. Okay, yeah, I get you. Your shifter friend is in a *very* bad way." He paused a moment. "Look, Ember, he's an old dude. Lived a long, full life. Maybe it's his time."

"It's not his time!" And he wasn't *old*. Age didn't apply to him.

"Then you have to get him—and yourself—to me. I'll be ready for you. I'll do what I can. Call me when you're on your way."

"Fine. I'm coming." She hit end and looked at Thane's prone body helplessly.

How the heck was she going to get him out to the

car? He had to be over two hundred pounds. Drag him on a rug? She'd never felt more useless in her life.

But then she remembered *The Goddess* statue from his house, so serene and strong, full of power. *The Goddess* could get Thane out to the car, but of course, *she* was part dragon.

Emerson froze. *And goddammit, so am I.*

She crouched down and hunted for his keys in his pocket to make sure they were there. They were. "You hold on to these for us, okay?"

"Okay," she answered for him and she grabbed her purse. *All set.*

She pulled him back up to sitting and put his good arm over her shoulder. Gritting her teeth, she sought deep down inside herself for strength she simply *had* to possess. All her life she had been, as she was now, as strong as she'd needed to be. Dragons were like that.

She took a deep breath and a hot, slick tingling sensation ran over her skin and inside her bones. She stood up, power thrumming through her veins. Thane rose with her, his head hanging forward, his body smoldering in her grasp. She was Bloodkin and wouldn't ever deny it again.

She carried him to the car, maneuvered him into the passenger seat, and adjusted the back as far as it would go. She got in the driver side and set her phone on the dash beside her. She started the engine and put the car in gear.

Thane had driven fast, but she was about to see what an Audi R8 could really do.

* * *

"…COUNTED FIVE OF THEM down there," Ember was saying, her voice floating like a wayward balloon in Thane's mind. "Why is your Alpha being such a jerk about us?"

"He's a jerk, period," a male voice said. "But the pack has to obey him."

"Has to?" Ember asked. Thane latched on to her voice like a lifeline.

"His being Alpha includes a…compulsion thing that's very hard to fight," the male said. "But it's possible to break free, which is why I'm going lone wolf as soon as your situation is resolved and you're safe."

Her safety was *Thane's* problem, not this stranger's, but the word *wolf* sparked something in Thane's memory. What had dragons to do with wolves? Something important.

"I have to find a new place to live, anyway," Ember said. "You can stay with me, and when Sadie gets better, she can join us. It'll be like old times."

No, this wolf could not *stay with her.*

Thane wrestled with the weight pinning him in

darkness, but the effort made pain flower in his chest, his heartbeat bouncing wildly. He took a deep breath to quiet it, and an unpleasant odor, like wet fur, filled his nostrils. And the pallet upon which he lay was very hard and lumpy. Not his bed. Not his stronghold.

"Thane?" Ember's voice was very close now. Fingertips softly brushed his face, and he hoped they belonged to her. "Only you could take a Drachentöter and live to tell the tale."

The darkness in his mind rushed into a cyclone of memory.

Drachentöter. Vampire. Lena.

Lena had known about Carreen and Rinc all along. She might have even killed them. He'd gone to her for answers but had been met with another assassin. He'd fought in a house already filled with death, and he'd sent Ember in deeper…after a whispered voice.

"Godric," Thane said, opening his eyes.

"There you are," Ember said, smiling down at him. She was wearing a man-sized green T-shirt. Thane turned his head toward the source of the offensive smell and found a Wolfkin watching him. *Right. Bryan, her foster brother.*

"I can't believe you're alive," the wolf said. "I would've put you out of your misery, but Ember is crueler than I am."

Ember was Bloodkin. "Where am I?" Thane asked.

He tried to sit up, but his shoulder roared with pain and his heart pounded so hard that stars gleamed in his vision. Ember pushed him back down again, and he allowed it. He looked around the space as he lay there. He was in a small room, too claustrophobic for a dragon's comfort, dingy and cluttered with books. It reminded him of a ship's cabin from long ago. He'd been undressed at some point and now wore only sweatpants and a gauze bandage on his shoulder.

"We're at Bryan's place in Santa Barbara," Ember said. "I didn't dare go back to your house after everyone at Lena's had been murdered. I figured Bryan's place would be safe, although *safe* is a relative term. Half his pack is prowling the street below this building. His Alpha isn't happy that one of his wolves is in league with dragons."

"That's because your brother's association with us challenges his Alpha's authority," Thane said absently. He lifted the arm of his injured shoulder and flexed the hand. A deep ache barked at the movement, but it wouldn't be long before he had its full use again.

"My sister is royalty," the wolf told him.

Thane grunted in agreement. He could deal with the wolf's smell if he felt that way about Ember. Thane met her gaze. "Have you contacted Matthew?"

Matthew would have some clothes ready for him.

"He hasn't picked up his phone for the past two

days," Ember said.

"Two days?" Thane made to sit up again, and this time he managed to get himself upright. "Try him again. Now."

Ember sighed, but she pulled her mobile from her back pocket. She put it on speaker and dialed. The call rolled to voicemail.

She shook her head at Thane. "I'm sorry. I'm hoping he was able to get out of your house before any trouble started, and just left his phone behind. He doesn't know to look for us here."

Left his phone—? Matthew was inseparable from his mobile. He would never leave it behind. The alternative scenario was that he was still at the house. Unable to answer. A vision of Matthew collapsed in his own blood floated before Thane's eyes.

He tried to stand. "We have to go. He may yet be alive."

Decades of dragon blood might have sustained him. He'd been injured many times in the past. There was still hope.

"You're barely conscious," Ember said. "I think we need to wait until you're better in case another creepy killer is waiting for you at your house. You're in no shape to fight again."

"This is *Matthew*," Thane told her.

"I know. But you look like you're going to fall over,"

Ember shot back. "You've been lucid for all of two minutes. You almost died on me."

"He'd do it for me, Ember. He *has* done it for me." *So many times.*

"I can go," Bryan said to Thane. "Now that you're awake, you can hold off Ray—he's my asshole Alpha." He looked over at Ember. "Ray doesn't have the balls to attack Thane Ealdian."

Thane was taken aback by the wolf's generosity. "I would be most grateful. Matthew is family."

"You've been taking care of my girl," Bryan said. "I'm happy to do it."

"You've got to be kidding," Ember said to Bryan. "That last killer…he was like a big insect on the wall. He almost killed *Thane*."

"Not an insect. Vampire," Thane said under his breath.

Bryan nodded as if he'd guessed as much, but Ember's eyes widened in horror as she mouthed the word *vampire*.

"Oh please, Ember," Bryan said, shrugging off the danger. "Give a wolf some credit. I may not be shifter royalty, but I can handle myself. I'll do a little sniffing around and report back. Easy."

His tone was disarming, and Thane could see Ember's resolve wavering.

"If you get hurt," she said, "I swear I will make you

miserable."

"Noted." The Wolfkin didn't seem afraid.

"And thank you," she added.

Thane reached out to clasp the wolf's hand. "You know where to go?"

"Yeah, Ember told me where you live. Just don't let Ray near her," Bryan said, "or he'll try to prove something to the rest of the pack."

"I wish this Ray would try," Thane said. Even injured, he could take a wolf.

Bryan put on a leather jacket. He looked like something of a rascal and had the wiles to go with it. When this was over Thane might just have work for him.

"How about you worry about Godric," Bryan said, "and I'll take care of Ray when you both are set."

"Call if you find anything," Ember said. "Call if you don't, too."

Bryan left the apartment with a nonchalant wave over his shoulder. He was a good man; Thane approved of Ember thinking of him as kin. The fact that the wolf acted brotherly was a relief, and Ember had bickered at him like a sibling, as well.

Ember moved to the window again and trained her gaze below. Thane pushed to his feet and came to stand next to her. Yes, some four stories down, there were men under the streetlights prowling like wolves and crouched on street benches. At least twenty by his count, light occasionally reflecting eerily in their eyes. He wondered how Bryan would evade them, but he didn't doubt that he would.

"How long until he reaches my stronghold?" Santa Barbara to Big Sur. Thane didn't know how to gauge modern transportation times anymore.

"I'd guess about four hours, maybe more," she said, leaning in to the glass. Then she pointed upward. "Look!"

Thane lifted his gaze in time to see a male silhouette land on a neighboring rooftop, crouch low, and creep to the other side of the building. Thane grinned in satisfaction. The pack wouldn't be able to catch Bryan. Thane absolutely had work for him.

He dismissed the threat below and turned to Ember. "Tell me everything."

"I don't want to," she said, an ache in her voice. "You're hurt already. Can it be enough that Godric is the bad guy? How about you kill him—or I will—and then forget the past?"

She was offering to kill one of the Triad? She, who was so opposed to bloodshed?

"I appreciate the offer," he said wryly, "but I need to know. Lena did this to me, didn't she?"

Ember faced him and opened her hands as if she wanted to give him something—solace maybe—but her palms were empty. "I think her intentions... Well, they weren't good, but they weren't all bad, either."

"Just tell me, Ember. Do me that courtesy. I've waited so long for it."

Her eyes welled with tears, and she pressed her lips together, as if refusing one last time. "Carreen was unfaithful to you…with Godric."

Thane drew back slightly. He'd known she'd taken a lover at some point and he'd also known that Carreen hadn't been happy in the marriage. The religious rhetoric of the time was that shifters were demon-born, and that God favored meekness in women. He never should've laughed at her. He should've listened. Nevertheless, she'd done her duty, and he'd done his. Their marriage had joined two lands, creating a great swath of open country within which the dragons of their bloodlines could fly. It was a union many had feared, so much power coming together as one.

The surprise was that *Godric Tredan* had been the one to touch his wife. Godric of the Triad. He'd been an *ally*. He'd visited the Ealdian stronghold on many occasions. Visited and…?

Thane closed his eyes against the thought.

"And Lena said she'd helped Carreen in that regard," Ember said. "Helped her meet with him."

So *both* Carreen and Lena had conspired to deceive him. The pain in his shoulder muted, another kind of hurt bruising through his body. "Go on."

She paled. "She said Rinc wasn't yours."

All the air in the room went rotten, poisonous to breathe. *"What?"*

She nodded. "Lena was pretty unintelligible near the end, but she tried very hard to tell me this… Godric was the father. And he killed both of them."

Godric was the father. Of all the scenarios that had played out in Thane's mind, this had not been one of them. The story Ember told was so simple, but he couldn't understand it. The pieces of the puzzle were all laid out, and they *appeared* to snap together so easily, and yet he couldn't make them fit. *Wouldn't* make them fit. Not those pieces.

"I'm so, so sorry, Thane. I can't imagine how terrible—"

Sound rushed his head, blocking out everything else. "Rinc wasn't mine?"

"We'll go after Godric," she said. "We'll track that bastard down and shove one of those slayer spears through his heart. I'll do it myself. With pleasure. He doesn't deserve to live after all the blood he's spilled. His own son. He killed his own son."

"*My* son," Thane said. The pain of losing Rinc again, losing him *this* way, was agony beyond anything he'd known. He'd easily take another Drachentöter in its place.

"Your son," Ember repeated, tears spilling down her

cheeks. "Of course."

CHAPTER 11

Ember stood by Thane as he stared out the window, his expression scarred by the agony of what he'd just learned. He didn't move. Barely breathed. She held her breath with him.

Minutes ticked into an hour and then two, but he still didn't move and neither did she. She wasn't leaving him alone with his new, terrible knowledge. If she thought he'd be receptive, she'd have wrapped her arms around him and held him tight. But it was as if he'd turned to stone. Night fell and deepened to an ominous, obsidian black, and she didn't budge from his side.

When her mobile rang, she merely lifted it to her ear,

ready for the worst.

"Matthew is probably okay," Bryan said on the other line.

Thane turned his head slightly toward her, and she put the phone on speaker so that he could hear more easily. "What do you mean *probably*?" she asked.

"I'm told he went looking for you and Thane with someone named Nerea Herrera. They left someone behind at Thane's place in case you guys returned here. Nice spread, by the way. Little cramped for my taste. And the view—all that ocean—must get real dull."

It was not the time to be funny. "Why isn't Matthew answering his phone, then?" she asked.

"I don't know." Bryan sounded weary. "Is it okay if I tell this *very insistent* person where you guys are, so that they can tell the other Herrera people?"

Ember looked over at Thane, who gave a curt nod of his head. "They're your allies. I'm guessing they finally want to make contact with you."

"Yes, go ahead," she said to Bryan, frowning at the word *allies*. What a joke. "That's fine." The faster Matthew could come to them, the better. She wished he were a dragon so he could fly straight here. Maybe he'd know what to say to Thane, what would help him. Had she made a mistake in passing on Lena's message?

No, she'd do it again. He deserved to know. He'd always deserved to know.

"Where is Matthew now?" she asked.

Bryan repeated the question to someone on his end, and she heard an answering murmur. "Evidently, they thought you might be in New York City."

"Where the Triad meets," Thane said with a bitter curl to his mouth.

This was a disaster.

"Okay," she said to Bryan. It'd be a while, then. "You better stay away from here. I count twenty Wolfkin on the street now."

"Sounds like a party." His voice had gone light. "I'll be back as soon as I can."

* * *

WITH THE PASSING OF the hours, the ache had diminished in Thane's shoulder and his breathing had eased, his heartbeat returning to normal. He inhaled deeply, feeling his lungs expand, blood quickening in his veins, his senses sharpening.

He could smell Ember's stress, but she hadn't moved. He'd wanted a loyal and steadfast woman, and despite blood and fire, here she was. He should lighten her heart.

"Ember," he said.

She looked at him, circles under her dragon-green eyes.

"Lena was wrong," he said. "Rinc *was* my son. I know

it. I can still see him. He *felt* like my son. My dragon *knew* him."

And he didn't think the dragon could be fooled. That part of him had *never* been uncertain of anything. The dragon was absolute, and it hadn't wavered now, not even with Ember's tearful confession. It was Thane the man who'd feared the worst. He'd simply needed time to let the fear pass and the truth reassert itself in his heart. There had been something…undeniable, *immutable* between him and his son. Rinc had been an Ealdian. Carreen might've felt that, too, had she not repudiated that deeper, elemental part of herself. But she had, and so she'd been wrong, and in turn, Lena had been wrong.

Godric was not Rinc's father. And *that* had to be why Godric had killed him.

"I could've misunderstood her," Ember said. But the wistfulness in her voice told him that she'd understood what Lena had said all right.

He sighed. "I acknowledge the possibility that Carreen *could've* carried Godric's child, but she didn't. The truth stands: Carreen bore my son, and she tried to shift in order to save him. Godric will pay."

"Just Godric? Not his heir?"

Thane fisted his right hand and flexed it again. His stomach growled. "He doesn't have one anymore. His son died during World War I."

"Lucky him," she said.

Thane grinned at her, then laughed out loud. "Don't be so sad, Ember."

"I was sad with you," she said defensively. "I was going to be sad with you as long as it took."

"Isn't it better that Rinc *did* belong to me?"

"Well, yeah." Her eyes were getting wet again. "But you've been thinking that for a while now, and here I've been worrying..."

Thane couldn't help himself. He cupped her face and pressed his mouth to her lips. He tried to be gentle, with all his willpower he tried, but he was not a gentle man. He had never been. He wanted to inhale her, consume her, taste and touch every inch of her so that both the dragon and the man were satisfied. Bloodkin were not known for moderation.

She trembled for a moment—*frightened?*—but then she moaned and her arms went around him, one of her hands fisting his hair to bring him even closer to her.

He chuckled against her lips, and she backed suddenly, a little line of worry between her brows. "Are you okay? Did I hurt you?"

Finally, a woman made for him. "No. Never. Sweetheart, I dare you to try."

"You *were* almost fatally wounded."

"It was a scratch," he said. "Now, please, I beg you, take that ugly shirt off. I want to smell you, not that shaggy dog."

171

She grinned, a flicker of fire in her eyes. "Don't let him hear you call him that."

In one movement, she lifted the shirt from her body, but his view was still obstructed by a female undergarment, a thing of torture if there ever was one—for both parties. Why did women insist on such restrictive contraptions?

"You sure you're okay?" she asked.

He gathered her to him, the bare skin at her waist like satin under his hands.

"Not okay," he murmured against her neck. "Not by a long shot. But ask me again in few hours."

* * *

EMERSON ARCHED HER BACK in Thane's arms, eyes wide with surprise as he grazed his teeth along her collarbone. She hadn't thought this through. Maybe she should've asked a few questions. Because the man's hands *scorched* where they roamed—rounding over her hips, under the waistband of her borrowed sweatpants, and over her ass—but the burn didn't hurt so much as it made her nerves crackle with feeling. He was a match; she was flint. And between them both…fire.

Her vision shifted and went strange, color so bright and vivid that she had to close her eyes for a moment. The world washed dark red, but it didn't matter. The craving that rose so fierce and fast within her intensified *all* her senses so that she ignored Thane's attempts to release her bra. If she didn't breathe him in *right now*, she thought she might die. She brushed her cheek along his chest to take his rich, dark, smoky scent inside her lungs.

She knew she was not being sexy or cool, but how could she play cool if she was so damn hot?

And she had to taste him… But he was wrestling with her pants, so she contented herself by moving her open mouth across his pecs, her tongue and teeth rasping across the tight skin under a smattering of chest hair.

Not enough. Not nearly enough.

She had to go *lower*, and was just sinking when he moved, stroking a hand deep into her hair and pinning her against him.

"Little dragon," he said. "You'd feel better if we worked *together*."

A sob of frustration broke from her throat. "I thought I knew how to do this," she said. But all the feelings were too strong, the drives overwhelming. She had to get his pants off. Now. But he was holding her too tightly to get at what she wanted.

"I think I'm dying," she told him. This ache would kill her.

He chuckled. "No, you're merely awakening. And I'm going to show you how to fly."

Merely? She wasn't *merely* anything. She'd known the

Bloodkin were dangerous, and Thane was the deadliest of all. She was about to be ruined, utterly and completely ruined, and yet, all she could say was, "Yes, please."

He tilted her face up to him, and she opened her eyes to find his indigo gaze upon her. He fit his mouth to hers in a rough slide and lock, and then took her deep into black velvet ecstasy. She tasted him, relishing him like the darkest of chocolate—yes, *this* was what she'd wanted, all her senses engaged at once—and knew that she could survive on kisses alone, and ever be satisfied.

His previous efforts proved genius when he lifted her against him, and she discovered that they were both naked. Her legs straddled his waist, breasts heavy with sensation, her core flush with his belly.

He laid her down on the bed he'd occupied during the four days of his recovery. His weight slid up her body, and the friction of contact rippled like flame across her skin. Fire didn't hurt. Fire loved her. And she loved fire. It's what she was made of. She knew that now.

With the realization, strength and power flowed through her, a strange tingling in her bones. She was brand-new and ancient, desire and rage, woman and dragon—all simultaneously.

"Ember," Thane said, forcing her to meet his eyes by touching her chin with his hand. "This is *not* the time for shifting."

"But I want *everything*," she said, yet didn't recognize

her near-feral voice. She trapped one of his legs with hers, knotting them together. His erection was a large firebrand on the inside of her thigh.

"And so you will, my lady." He nuzzled her neck, a gesture more primal than human, before letting go of her chin to stroke and cup her breast, his thumb massaging her nipple. "Just hold on. Hold on to me."

The longing was excruciating, even cruel, but when Thane pushed inside her, filling her so completely, the blood in her veins turned to molten gold, melting her worries away with each beat of her heart. His possession set off a chain reaction through her system, each cell flaring with sensation, the heat of magic a transformative force that might not have turned her into a dragon, but nevertheless, changed her forever.

She curled around him as he moved, his rhythm slow like the tempo of an ocean, but just as absolute and unrelenting. She sensed her climax coming when it was still a long way off, so that by the time the wave reached her, she crested so high and so long that she indeed felt like she was flying.

When she could see again, she realized the gift he'd given her. Strain etched across his brow, his skin just slightly darker than his human self. He moved with greater force—a second swell of feeling filling her—and he growled as he found his release. She clutched him to her as they shuddered, drawing him as deep as she could.

And when he collapsed on top of her, she contented herself by licking a drip of sweat that was winding down his neck.

She waited—generously, she thought—until he got his first full breath before saying, "I think we have to do it again."

"Yes, love," he said, his voice warm with humor. "That was just to take the edge off. We'll be at this awhile."

* * *

"YOU DON'T NEED TO do that," Thane said, exasperated. "I can hire someone to come." She was *his lady*; she didn't need to be doing common chores.

"Oh yes, I do. Bryan's going to be back any minute." Ember shoved the sheets in the small upright washing machine, dropped a blue cube inside, slammed the lid, and gave a dial a twist. "And open the window, please."

Thane had readily agreed to the shower sex. He'd loved how the water evaporated from their bodies into hissing steam as they'd coupled, but part of him wanted the wolf to know what had transpired while he'd been gone so that there could be no confusion—ever—about what Ember was to Bryan and what she was to Thane.

He needed to talk to her about their new situation, but she threw a pair of the wolf's athletic pants at his head. Thane's own clothes had been too ruined from the vampire attack to be salvageable.

"Put those on," she said.

He needed to tell her that she belonged to him, and he needed her to acknowledge it absolutely by accepting his ring on her finger, and soon. She was the woman he wanted. They could get to know each other's nuances better in time. Courtship was highly overrated.

But he kept silent because that was exactly what had happened with him and Carreen and their arranged marriage. Ember was a modern woman who had professed often, and with feeling, how she wanted her independence from the Bloodkin. Words of possession might make her run away from him. Matthew had warned that it would.

Thane needed a strategy.

"Pants," she said, smiling too-sweetly, as if to make him hurry. "You put your feet down each leg and pull them up."

Just for that, he balled the pants, threw them to the side, and advanced on her. She wore only a towel, her hair a mess of wet waves. She smelled too sweet again. A little sweat would make everything better.

"No, no, no," she said, laughing as she backed away. "There's no time for that, and you know it."

He grinned. "Dragons have all the time they want."

"Not now they don't. You've got problems, buddy.

Serious problems."

"And isn't it wonderful that I have a solution, as well." He was getting hard again. It was good to be alive, and even better to be in her company. His dragon had ceased fighting him, content again after so long. He felt light, strong, and so pleased with himself.

"Well, you can just put your *solution* away," she said, trapping herself in the small galley that served as a kitchen. Her skin was rosy and golden, and nothing was prettier on her than the happy smile beneath her dragon-green eyes. If he was very careful, he might just get her to reassess her opinions of the Bloodkin, living like one, living *with* one.

He lunged for her, but she squealed and scrambled up on the counter, dodging around him. He snagged her towel as it flapped behind her, so he achieved half his goal anyway. Now to catch her…

But she'd paused, looking out the window. She crossed her arms over her lovely breasts and frowned deeply at the street below, her body going still with tension.

Damn. What now? Those wolves were such a nuisance.

He joined her and surveyed the area, the pavement glowing slightly yellow in the early morning sunlight. A car passed, but the pack was gone. And so, apparently, was the last of the morning's interlude with Ember.

"Call Bryan," he said, deciding once and for all that he

needed a phone of his own. He was ready to concede that battle to Matthew.

It'd been a half hour since Bryan's last call, the one that had driven Ember out of Thane's arms and into a cleaning frenzy. Bryan should be back, and in another hour at most, Matthew and the Herrera people would arrive, too.

"Do you think they went out to get pancakes?" she asked, punching at the face of her mobile angrily.

No, he did not. The Alpha had surely found a way to trap or intercept their renegade pack member.

"He's not picking up," she said.

Thane kissed her temple. "We'll find him. The Wolfkin scent is very…distinctive. We'll have no trouble tracking them."

She didn't laugh, as he'd hoped, but turned away to return the pile of clothes she'd dug out of one of Bryan's drawers. "Do you have good lawyers?"

"I have the best lawyers." He retrieved the athletic pants and chose a T-shirt from the pile. "Why?"

"If they hurt my brother," she said, shoving her legs into her skirt and zipping it up, "I'm going to commit murder."

She was a dragon all right, through and through.

"I'll bribe the judge and get you off," he said gamely, though he would never allow any of those wolves near her. He reached for his shoes—one was crusty with blood, a testament to how much he'd lost during the encounter with the vampire.

They were out the door in short order.

Indeed, a pack of wild dogs was *not* hard to follow. Their scent was earthy, their sweat slightly sharper to the nose than that of humans, and many had not showered for the long days of their watch beneath Bryan's apartment.

Thane set off down the street that led toward the sun. He could almost *see* their scent in the air. Even Ember made the first turn without waiting for his signal, and from there, he let her lead. A garbage truck momentarily confused her and she stalled in the center of an intersection, but then she pointed down State Street, and he nodded.

He heard the growls long before she looked over at him, worry rounding her eyes. But it was the note of blood in the air that really concerned him. Ember took off her heels—the only footwear she had with her—and in her bare feet ran toward the sound of violence.

They caught up with them in a parking lot near Mission Creek, next to an unfinished construction site, rebar sticking up out of concrete columns like lightning rods.

The Wolfkin pack—some thirty males and females, several in wolf form—had made a circle around two shirtless fighters at its center. Ray and Bryan stalked each other, dust and sweat creating patches of brown grit on their skin. One of the wolves in the outer circle had pissed nearby, the acidic smell mixing with the back-alley funk. The Wolfkin's heartbeats drummed rapidly, all out of sync, creating a cacophony of savagery.

Bryan was bleeding from his side, and a dimpled welt on his skin said his lower ribs were likely broken.

Ember started to rush forward, but Thane held her back. "Let him fight."

"He's hurt!" she said, struggling futilely in his hold.

Yes, Bryan was hurt. Badly. Thane didn't like how he was favoring his injured side.

Ray took advantage, taunting Bryan with his jaw out and his hands down. "You're weak. Always been weak. Always will be weak."

"It's the Wolfkin way," Thane said low in her ear. "This is an Alpha fight. Whoever wins controls the pack."

Which was why dragons thought it was much better to choose leaders in Assembly. And not so long ago, he would've agreed with them. But Godric was one of the Triad and he'd shed so much blood that now Thane considered that the Wolfkin way might be better. A single fight to the death and the matter was decided.

"But I just got him back," Ember said, her voice loaded with anxiety.

Bryan circled Ray to the left, and Ray tracked him,

feinting while looking for the best angle to jab at Bryan's injury.

"Give your wolf a chance," Thane said. "He's clever. Biding his time. I think he can win."

"He doesn't even want to be Alpha," she told him. "He wants to go lone wolf."

"Maybe becoming Alpha is the only way he can."

Bryan had finally had enough of Ray's taunts, and with surprising speed, he lunged at him, trying to pin him against a low concrete wall. But Ray was ready, and he managed to get ahold of Bryan's neck...momentarily. In one smooth motion, Bryan swept Ray's leg out from under him and brought his weight down, flipping Ray over and slamming him to the ground. Ray recovered quickly, but when he rolled and stood up, Bryan caught him with a swift, hard kick to the face.

Ray limply fell back in the dust as Bryan collapsed onto his knees, one arm awkwardly winged at his side. Blood frothed at his mouth. He was the victor, but also easy pickings for the next wolf who dreamed of being Alpha. Which looked like all of them.

"Can I go help now?" Ember asked Thane.

He nodded. "Now would be good."

She ran to the circle, battering a male out of her way, who growled viciously at her. Thane stalked calmly behind her. His dragon was showing in his eyes, in the hulking of his shoulders, and the itch of his thickening claws. He lashed out at the growling Wolfkin—*no one threatened Ember*—and the dog yelped.

Bryan's head was in her lap, his body broken, something crushed in his spine, as well. He trembled, but gritted his teeth against the pain.

Ember didn't look up when she asked, "How do I do it?"

Thane knew what she meant, though the Assembly had a law prohibiting sharing dragon blood with other types of shifters. But Bryan was her brother, too; he was kin, family, and that's exactly what Thane would argue when defending her before the Triad.

He knelt down beside her and took her forearm in his grasp. With the pad of his thumb, he sought for a good spot on her vein, and then he pierced her soft skin with his nail. She didn't whimper or recoil, but the green in her eyes shined brighter than ever. Always the brave one.

"I have to keep hold"—he pressed steadily with the point of his nail—"or you'll heal too quickly."

"Okay," she said. "Whatever he needs."

Deep-red blood, rich with old magic, trickled across her wrist. She brought her arm near Bryan's mouth, and though his eyes flickered back in their sockets and he choked with pain, she let her blood drip between his parted lips.

The growling around them got louder and angrier, but when Thane cast a lazy glance over his shoulder—*please, try me*—the pack quieted into frightened whimpers.

"He'll live?" Ember asked as the drips became a narrow stream.

"Longer than usual," Thane replied. Bryan might also experience some unpleasant side effects, but that couldn't be helped. What Ember wanted, Thane would make happen. And she wanted Bryan to live.

She smiled shakily at Thane, relief in her eyes. And then her gaze shifted over his shoulder, and her expression sobered. "Who's that?"

Thane turned, and his dragon nearly blacked his mind with sudden bloodlust.

"Godric," Thane ground out. The stink and noise of the wolves had disguised his approach. For the first time, Thane could see what had drawn Carreen to him: the angled set of Godric's dragon eyes made him appear more fae than beast. His irises were a pale blue color that gleamed in contrast to his moonlight-silver hair. Someone *might* think he was gentle, like a poet. Poor Carreen. She should've known better.

How had he known where they were? Had the Herreras told him? Possibly. Thane glanced at Ray's corpse. Or maybe the dead Alpha had contacted the Triad complaining of dragons in their territory. Either way, it seemed this trap set for Bryan had been a trap for dragons, as well.

A clever trap. So clever that Thane could feel the cage

shutting around him. There was no way he could win...or win everything.

As a dragon, Godric could easily overpower any man, including a Bloodkin. And if Thane shifted to fight, he'd be too feral, too mindless, to shift back, and thereby he'd lose Ember. And then Godric could claim that Thane's dragon had ascended, and Godric was forced to put him down, just as Thane had done with Gerard. *Very clever.*

"Want me to kick his ass?" Ember asked. "I'm pretty sure I can. Lemme try."

Thane smiled at her. She would've made him so happy.

"I would," he said, looking down at her, "but Matthew would have my head. He's very old-fashioned."

"Uh-huh," she said dryly, as if she knew something was awry. "Sure he is."

Godric had killed Carreen and Rinc, and now Thane was going to die, too. At least he was going to take Godric with him.

He winked at Ember and stood, his body blocking her from Godric's view. "Hello, old friend," he called out. "Isn't this convenient?"

Chapter 12

"You're a hard man to kill, Thane," Godric said. "The closest I've been able to come is to let time have its way with you, but then time burped up those bodies from the very bowels of the earth and here we are again."

Emerson's mind was hopping through the implications of Godric appearing here and now, and she'd come to one conclusion: he had one-upped Thane with a damned-if-you-do-damned-if-you-don't scenario. Thane couldn't win against a dragon unless he shifted himself. Sneaky.

"Perhaps it's fated that we meet," Thane said. "You

took a coward's way by going after my wife and child, and now you must face me."

She glanced down to find the skin on her wrist now unbroken, blood drying in a dark trickle down the curve of her arm. Bryan had gone silent, his pallor chalky, so either he was dead or healing, but she couldn't afford the moment to check which one. She gave his hand a little squeeze as a prayer and felt his fingers twitch inside her grasp. *Thank God.* The rest of the Wolfkin had retreated slightly, glued to the spectacle before them.

Godric laughed. "I never cared about you," he said. "I wanted Carreen and her land. She had been intended for *me* until her father got greedy and wanted to form a dragon dynasty with the Ealdian blacks. So I *took* what should've been mine." He shrugged. "And I disposed of what wasn't."

He meant Rinc. Which made Emerson's skin heat with rage. A baby. Innocent. Helpless. Thane's.

"Carreen got upset about that," he said with a dramatic sigh. "We quarreled. It didn't end well."

Okay, Emerson *really* didn't like this Godric guy. Someone needed to take steps to see to his speedy removal from this earth. She'd always wanted to perform a public service but had never found the time. And she certainly wasn't going to sit back and let the boys duke it out—to Thane's ultimate disadvantage. Because, hello, she was a dragon, too. Or was Godric so pigheaded that he didn't think she would fight?

She stood and brushed the dirt from her skirt.

"Ah, *Emerson*," Godric said proudly. "I would know you anywhere."

Her head ached and spun, as if she'd been hit in the face.

His words echoed in her ears—*would know you anywhere*—and she shivered, recognizing the sentiment behind them.

Please, no. Because that would just suck.

Statements like that and the pride behind them were the stuff of orphan fantasies—having the eyes or the smile or the coloring of some long-lost relative—when in reality, the relative often turned out to be a total shit. Ember wouldn't have spared it a moment's thought, except his uttering the orphan line had also answered the final question left hanging with Lena's death: what the hell did Emerson have to do with anything?

She could take a pretty good guess now. She might be an Emmerich Red, but somehow she had Godric's blood in her, too.

"Ember," Thane said, "get away."

"Don't tell me what to do," she cut back. She was busy grappling with her total-crap heritage. She'd gone from nobody, to royalty, to spawn in the space of ten days. She just really wanted to be Ember. Ember Clark. Was that so much to ask?

"This is between me and him," Thane said.

She kinda wished it was, but nothing was that easy.

"And what if I'm his heir?" she asked Thane. Because he'd sworn over and over again to avenge both Carreen and Rinc by taking the lives of both the murderer and his heir. Godric's son might've died, but she bet she was next in line.

Thane turned her way, horror blanching his skin white. Yeah, he'd slept with the enemy. Like five times in one day. Actually, the sheets probably needed to go into the dryer now.

"Come stand by me," Godric said, lifting an arm to her in welcome. "I swear on the Tredan bloodline that I didn't know about you. That I would've come for you."

The Bloodkin had a thing about blood. It was all-powerful, the ultimate connection. Now, more than ever, she was glad she wasn't really one of them.

"Why should I believe you?" She couldn't be too eager.

"Because you are a dragon," he said fiercely. "Inside, you must have always known you were set apart, that you were born to fly, not scrabble in the dirt. I would've given you the world, but Lena, in her anger, kept you from me and gave you to Thane."

She lifted her chin and slid her gaze over to Thane. "Mr. Ealdian intends to kill you."

Godric smiled. "Mr. Ealdian died with his wife and

child. It's time he knew it."

"And then what?"

"And then the future is ours." He gestured impatiently with his hand. "Come!"

She thought of *The Goddess* in Thane's home and let tranquility loosen her shoulders, giving her the heat of confidence when she should be quailing. But the truth was, Thane couldn't do this. Not alone.

Just a little bit closer. She walked over to Godric and said, "Take me home."

* * *

THANE CLOSED HIS EYES for a moment to recover his composure.

Lena had tried to be loyal, in her own way, after the fact. She'd given him Ember and had kept Ember's existence a secret from Godric, which had been *her* revenge for the murder of her sister and nephew. He could forgive Lena now.

"I sent two dragon slayers after him," Godric said to Ember.

"The vampire almost succeeded," she coolly told him.

"Occasionally, it's best to handle business yourself."

Thane had to work hard to conceal his awe. Ember was as cunning as any dragon ever. Godric was betting on blood, but she made her family where she wanted.

Blood had no claim on her—never had—and if Godric had taken one more minute to get to know her, he would've realized it, too.

Never trust a serene Ember.

Thane inhaled and stepped slightly back to survey the area for a weapon, an advantage, anything. The pack of angry wolves was gathered behind him. They'd started growling again, which could be good or bad, considering Bryan was still collapsed in the dirt. Rebar from the surrounding building demolition was exposed a half a block away. Some humans were watching from the rooftop, and far off, the wail of a police siren signaled the interference of human law.

"Have you shifted yet?" Godric asked Ember.

"No," she answered. "I don't know how."

He scowled. "Your dragon might have been stunted by your low upbringing. Watch and learn."

Thane breathed a sigh of relief when Bryan pushed himself up, his human body in a feral crouch. A ripple of power rolled over the remaining humans of the Wolfkin pack, as they were overtaken by spasms of change. Their clothes fell off in scraps as their bodies morphed into their more primal forms. Lines of blue and red were scrawled all over their skin until bristling hair covered them. Their teeth shined white, lips bared. Their ears were erect.

Bryan, the Alpha wolf, inclined his head slightly, as if

waiting for a signal.

It came from Godric, who burst into the flames of change. The shift was glorious as he writhed within an exquisite rose of fire, and then stretched into the sky like a shadow made of burnished silver. His wings, a latticework of scales, shimmered iridescently in the sun. A creature of legend, the dragon took to the sky, wings beating once, twice, and leaning into a circular glide. How Thane envied him that.

A sharp bark brought his attention back down to earth, first to Bryan, and then to Ember, whose eyes had gone full green under a protruding crown of bone. Her hands were fisted, fire licking her skin like a lover.

"Ember, stop!" Thane yelled.

She knew he couldn't risk shifting, so she was. Was she actually planning to fight? Never mind that she was twenty-five and Godric was at least eight hundred.

"No, sweetheart," he begged her. "You don't have to do this."

But her gaze was trained upward. The fire enveloping her body deepened to the color of passion. Her chest rose, as if inhaling, and an Emmerich dragon—red like blood, red like fury, red like dawn—was born. Her head was elegant, spines fanning away from her face. Her neck was long and graceful, wings reaching with strength. She was sex, power, and beauty in their most elemental forms, and with a single beat, she launched into the air.

She positioned herself between Thane and the lightning bolt that was Godric's Tredan Silver, her long sinuous body rippling with each lift and stroke. The silver hissed at her, and she screamed back at him, a primeval sound that made a car crash on the street below the airborne dragons. Godric dived to get her to move, but she didn't flinch. He feinted and almost got around her, but she rammed him with her bent head and sent him off course.

On the ground, Thane had stopped breathing, his heart frozen in terror.

It seemed as if the silver finally understood that she was *defending* his prey, because when next he dived, he did so with teeth bared to rip into her flesh. To teach her the hard way to respect her elders.

And suddenly, Thane was in the air, too, the transition from man to madness a mere blink of sizzling agony. His dragon was a black, the largest of their kind, and he rose like the cloak of death on the world. He heard screams below as human observers ran for cover, but they wouldn't be able to escape their doom. He was free! The dragon would take what he wanted. And right now, he wanted to split silver dragon skin and show the puny beast just who was king of the sky.

The red and silver dragons were twined in an aerial struggle, teeth at each other's necks. But when the Ealdian Black circled, wind lovingly caressing his long body, the two broke apart. The red dragon didn't flee, but the silver one stretched, trying to get away.

There was no contest, never had been.

The black sliced through the air and latched on to the silver. A spurt of salty-sweet blood ran over his tongue, and then he brought the beast down on the exposed rebar, iron spearing through its chest and belly. The concrete and steel wouldn't kill the silver dragon, but it would pin him to the ground.

One down. The black turned to go after the red dragon, launching back into the sky. But once high on sunlight, its warm rays sparkling over his scales, the rush for blood eased.

The Emmerich Red matched his speed, stroke for stroke, and he understood that she was his mate and would satisfy his lusts *differently.* The rage left his heart and the simmering pleasure of flight seeped again through his body, his mind clearing like the blue of day around him.

Together, the Ealdian Black and Emmerich Red looked down as the pack of wolves swarmed over the bulk of the silver dragon and finished him off.

And when a car arrived, and a slightly balding man with a short sword under his coat got out, the black dragon remembered himself. *Thane.*

And flying beside him was Ember, his lady. His love. She probably wanted to be held. Or he did. Didn't matter who wanted what, actually.

He glided down and stepped out of the air on a man's legs, easily in control. It seemed as if while Ember had been moving toward her destiny as a dragon, he'd been slowly remembering how to be man.

Matthew held out a cloth of deep blue, and Thane reached for it.

"It's for the lady," Matthew said, as if to scold.

"Oh, thank God." Ember said. Thane found her beside him, naked. Clothes never survived shifts. She gratefully accepted what turned out to be a silky robe. Matthew was always prepared…except he'd brought nothing for his lord to wear.

"There wasn't time for two stops," Matthew said. "When I heard about the Wolfkin fight on the news, I made the Herreras break all the traffic laws to get here as fast as possible."

The wolves were still feasting on Godric. They would be the strongest Wolfkin pack in history.

Ember nudged Thane. "We've got more company."

A dark car was parked at the edge of the construction site, and Ransom and Locke Heolstor stepped out. There would be no revenge for them at all. Godric was already dead and so was Lena.

The brothers walked over to the gory carcass, and the wolves backed off, heads lowering as they acknowledged the dragons in their midst. Ransom looked down at the dead beast for a long moment, then turned his back and returned to the car. Locke spit upon the remains of Godric Tredan and then joined his brother.

* * *

"YES, WE SENT THE messenger," Nerea Herrera said. "At great risk to ourselves, I might add."

The woman sitting before Emerson didn't look like she had risked anything. Ever. She was gorgeous— honey-olive skin, dark hair, dark eyes, all of her in a luster of health and well-being. Her blouse clung to her curves, and her skirt was slit to *there*, so that if she uncrossed her long legs, Emerson might just have an unwanted *Basic Instinct* moment. No, thank you.

Emerson folded her arms. "An e-mail or letter or, say, a telephone call would've been preferable."

But arguing wasn't going to turn back the clock. And really, all she wanted right now was to get away from people and put her head on a pillow. So much had happened that she felt like an anxiety attack was imminent. Maybe a long bath would help. The huge suite Matthew had arranged for her had a huge tub to match.

"Pah!" Nerea said. "While you were being watched? There had to be no connection to us."

Because *no connection* is the very definition of *ally*. Right. Meanwhile, a pack of wolves were in lockup—to be sprung in the morning, Thane had promised—because *Bryan* had protected her, supported her, and showed her what *kin* meant.

Emerson turned toward Thane and shot him a look of frustration. He drew her to him, and she put her head on his shoulder.

"What I don't understand," he said, "was how Ember ended up in the human social services."

Oh yeah. There was that.

Nerea lifted her hands dramatically. "It seemed the safest."

For whom? Emerson wondered.

"That murderer Godric was in the Triad. Emerson was to be kept away from his influence and interests at all costs. Keeping her out of the Bloodkin world seemed the best way."

Again, for whom?

"And then when you *so stupidly* announced your heritage to the Assembly for school money, of all things, I didn't know what to do." Nerea sounded shocked. Money didn't grow on trees. How did she think Emerson was going to pay for school?

Thane growled, and so Emerson took up the questioning again.

"Who is my mother?"

"Ah, your mother was Nova Emerson, and hers was Mazarine Emerson, one of Godric's paramours at the time of the Ealdian murders. She concealed her pregnancy from Godric and raised Nova in secret."

Nova. Emerson gripped Thane's arm. Her mother's name had been Nova. And her grandmother was Mazarine. But *ick* and *shudder* about Godric.

"And my father?" The panic pushing at Emerson's chest was unbearable, but she had to know.

"Taggart Ackerman. A *Green,* for God's sake. But the Emmerich blood was clearly dominant." Nerea sighed hugely as if Emerson had escaped the worst. "They died together in a train wreck in Japan. 1991, it was. You were left in the care of their servant, a Jillian Stevens, who was...*encouraged* financially to adopt you. And here you are, alive and well. So my plan succeeded after all, even when Lena Orvyn was so determined to expose you."

Emerson felt Thane's breath on her ear. "I'll do some inquiries," he said. "Find out if there are Ackerman relatives still alive."

She was concentrating on breathing. *In and out.* It was so damn hot in the suite.

Nerea's eyes opened wide. "Now. You're probably dying to hear about the hoard, which is of course—"

"I've got to go," Emerson said to Thane. "Can you finish here for me?"

She didn't wait for him to answer, just set off for the bathroom and locked herself inside. She splashed her face with cold water and then slowly lifted her eyes to the mirror. She found a dragon looking back at her. Her skin was so hot, her muscles so tense that she clenched her hands to keep…*something* from happening.

But the pressure was growing.

She peeled off her clothes—anything to get cooler.

She was on her knees, shaking with tension, when a knock sounded on the door. "Ember, they're gone."

"Just give me a minute," she called out. She didn't want Thane to see her like this.

"Ember, open the door."

"Not feeling so great here," she said to be clear. "Need privacy."

Because she was having a complete and utter meltdown. She was due, actually, considering the events of the past week or so. This was normal. A good cry would help, if she could find the tears.

A rattle at the door, and it opened, the doorjamb busted where the lock had been.

"Go away," she said, hiding her face.

But his arms came around her, and he lifted her into his lap. "I forgot what it was like after shifting for the first time."

"Is that what this is?" She wasn't sure she was ready to do the dragon thing again. The first time, she hadn't really thought about it. She'd been thinking of Thane, protecting him. "What do I do? Go to the roof? Jump off?"

He chuckled and stroked her hair away from her face. "I think the people of Santa Barbara have seen enough dragons for today. The Assembly doesn't permit shifting near human habitation, but as Godric broke the law first and you were defending us both"—he smiled at that—"you're not being held responsible."

She'd been all over the news—or at least her dragon had—and Dr. Buckley from the university had been giving interviews all day on his extensive knowledge of the Bloodkin. Any hope of secrecy was now destroyed. The Assembly was meeting, and she and Thane had been requested to attend.

"Yay…I think." She shivered against a burn coursing over her skin. "So I just wait this out?" Because that would be hell. She needed to get out of here. The roof actually seemed like a good idea.

"You could," he said, his voice deep and throaty as he skimmed a hand across her belly and lower. "But I can think of something better…something that will satisfy your dragon just as much."

CHAPTER 13

THANE HAD SECURITY COVERING nearly every inch of his house, but Emerson couldn't help but follow her nose down to the kitchens, dodging around the busy staff he'd hired for the occasion to find the creamy, rich, sugary smell of wonderfulness that had lured her from his bedroom.

She'd left him in a naked, facedown sprawl, dead center on the bed, his bare feet and shins hanging off the end. But for all his efforts—and they were godlike—she wasn't quite sated.

Like a thief, she glanced over her shoulder to see if anyone was watching and then nosed into the big fridge, where—*hallelujah!*—a beautiful cheesecake with sliced strawberries decorating the top was waiting for this afternoon's big celebration.

Now here was the dilemma: She *could* exercise some self-control and forego eating what she was sure was a perfect confection until the party, where she could share it with everyone else, or... Considering the fact that they were celebrating her debut, it might be more in keeping with the *spirit* of the occasion for her to *take* what she wanted. *Because...dragon.* Therefore, taking possession of the cheesecake would in fact be *honoring* the occasion, and by extension her guests and her host.

"Can I get you anything, my lady?"

Busted. She shut the fridge door and turned to face Matthew. "It has strawberries."

"It's eight o'clock in the morning."

Emerson blinked rapidly, thinking really hard. "Why is that relevant?"

Matthew's lips twitched. "How about I have Maria send you up a tray?"

"Maria?" That was a new name.

"The full-time, live-in pastry chef whom my lord Thane recently hired."

Emerson arched a brow. *Live-in.* "And why would he do that?"

She didn't officially live here, so why would he need the pastry chef to? Not that Emerson wouldn't have said *no* if Thane had asked her to move in, but he seemed to have issues with commitment—never brought up the future—but after the Carreen thing, Emerson guessed she understood. So she'd been looking for her own place nearby. She could give him time; apparently, she had a lot of it.

But this was an interesting development. "Maria."

"...will bring you a tray."

Still Emerson waited.

Matthew closed his eyes as if he were struggling for patience. "And it will have a slice of cheesecake upon it."

Emerson grinned, went up on tiptoe, and kissed his cheek. "You take such good care of me."

She couldn't wait until later when her surprise guest would arrive and she could introduce him to Matthew. Her guest had recently graduated from Harvard Law and had been recruited to work for the Bloodkin Assembly, where he'd just accepted a position. Apparently, *Douglas* Chandler, Matthew's great-great grandson, was pretty smart.

"It's my honor, my lady." He gestured toward the door. "Now, if you will...?"

Get out of everyone's way?

She spun around happily. "I will."

* * *

THANE GRINNED WHEN EMBER burst into the bedroom. She was glowing, head to toe, her hair wild from lovemaking, her green eyes dancing with firelight. She seemed to have an excessive amount of energy this morning, but he was comfortable in bed...and a little apprehensive at the same time. He'd been planning this for a while.

"We don't have to be up for a few hours yet," he said, wanting her all to himself a little longer.

"We do," she told him. "Breakfast is on its way."

She climbed up on the bed—and onto him—and kissed him loudly on the mouth. She pulled back slightly, and he gazed up into her face. She seemed to be in a very good mood.

"Might I suggest a time-honored solution?" She waggled her eyebrows. "Breakfast *in* bed?"

He took hold of her hips, sighing. "All right. I'll compromise."

"It's not a compromise," she said. "It's win-win."

"It's a distraction," he told her. "I wanted your full attention for a little while, and until tomorrow, I think this is our only opportunity." There was the party, the guests, and then as the sun set, a shift and a long, exultant flight, her official entrée into the Bloodkin life.

"My attention is all yours," she said. "Well, ninety-seven percent of it is. Three percent is impatient for cheesecake."

"I'll take what I can get." He smirked at her. "I have something for you."

"Oh?" She wiggled excitedly on top of him. He found himself getting...*excited*, too.

"For your first shift, it's traditional to give gifts to start your hoard."

She was already a very wealthy woman. The Herreras might have been lax about *her*—and he wasn't ready to let that go quite yet—but they had been meticulous with every Emmerich cent.

He twisted slightly and reached out to open a drawer in the bedside table. His heart was beating fast, skin heating with anticipation. He grabbed his gift and turned back to her with it hidden in his fist.

She was smiling brightly at him.

No going back. He'd waited as long as he could. Neither man nor dragon could wait a moment longer.

He turned his hand over, and in his palm was a smooth, gray stone.

She looked at it for a long moment and then went very still. Her face flushed, and her eyes misted, seeming to glow.

"From your first hoard?" she asked.

So she remembered. "The first stone I collected."

Did she understand what he was trying to say?

She wiped at tears as they slipped from her eyes, but he didn't know if that was a bad or good sign.

"This is too much! I don't have a safe place for it yet," she said. "Maybe you could hold on to it for me. Keep it with the others until I do?"

"No." His voice broke. His heart would soon, too, if she didn't take it from him. "It should be with you. It's important to me that it stays with you."

She tilted her head, her forehead wrinkling with thought. "Maybe, if it's okay with you, I could stay here with it?"

Relief broke over him, like dawn after a long, dark night.

"Yes. Please," he said. "I need that. I need you." He held the stone out. "Please. Take it."

She brushed at her tears again and then took the stone from him, saying, "I love you, too."

ABOUT THE AUTHOR

Erin Kellison is the *New York Times* and *USA Today* bestselling author of the Reveler serial, where dreaming turns dangerous. This year she delves into shifter romance with her Dragons of Bloodfire series. To find out more and to sign up for Erin's newsletter, please visit www.ErinKellison.com.

Printed in Great Britain
by Amazon.co.uk, Ltd.,
Marston Gate.